GIBBONS

or

One Bloody Thing After Another

being the discontinuous narrative
of an Australian family
in short stories,
including glass eyes, false mermaids,
inadvertent death, nuclear weapons,
and the accidental destruction
of the Sydney Opera House.

James Morrison

Orbis Tertius Press

Alberta, Canada

Cover design and interior layout by James Morrison

Cover and chapter illustrations by James Morrison; image on p78 uses elements of a photo by Charles01, under the Creative Commons Attribution-Share Alike license.

Contents page illustrations by Ella Morrison.

Set in Alegreya, IBM Plex Mono, HVD Edding 780, and Komika Display.

ISBN: 978-1-7781566-4-9

for Lisa and Ella

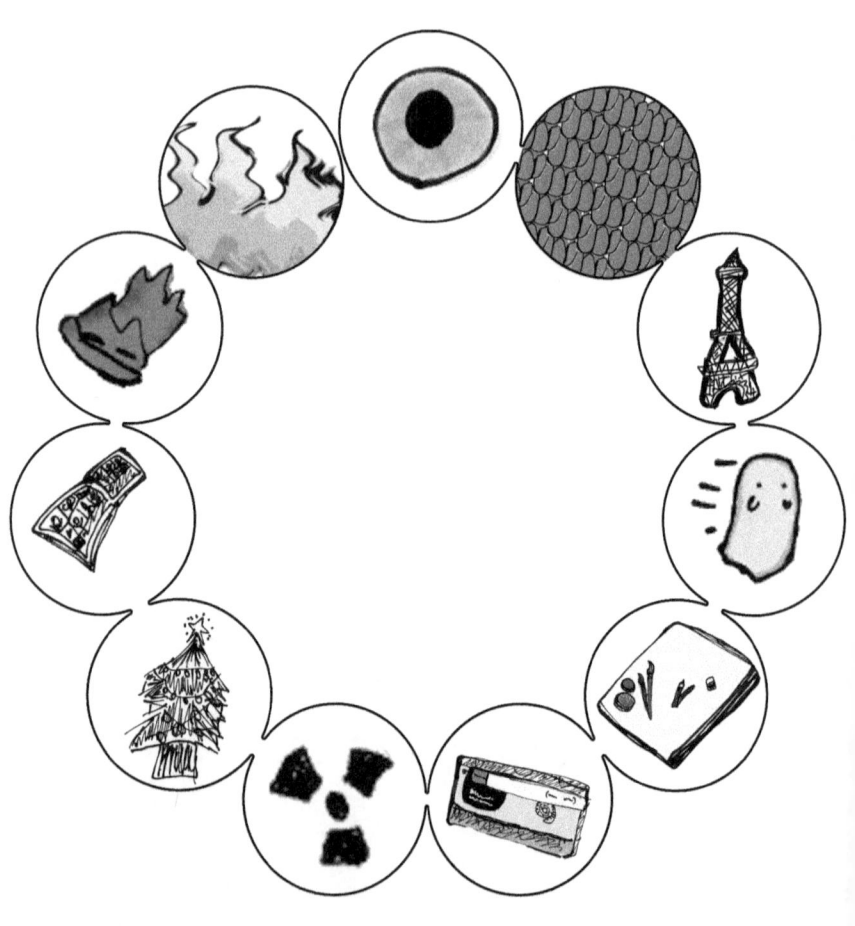

CONTENTS

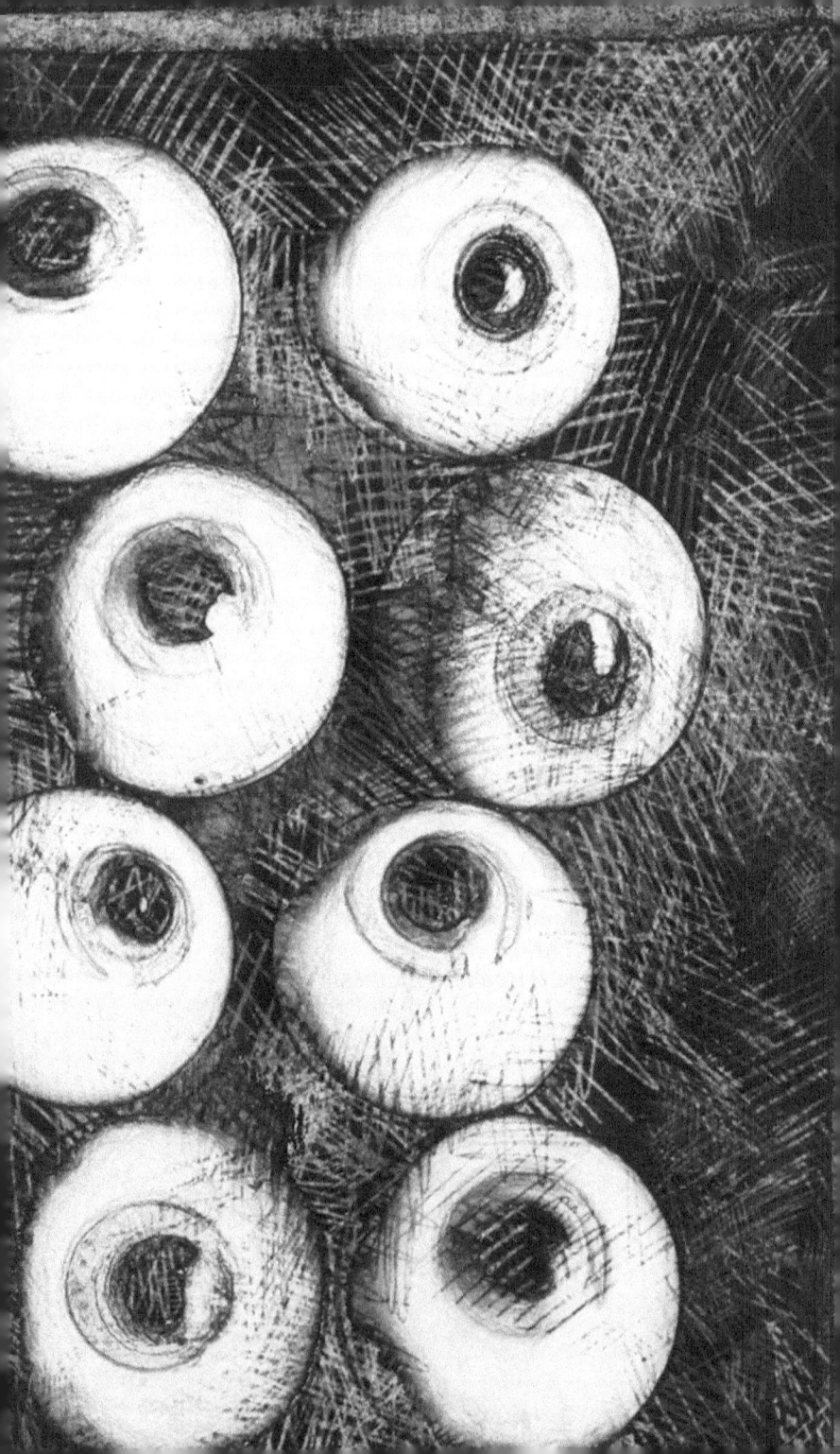

Eyes on a Wooden Floor

A shelf of eyes, polished and unblinking. At night Celeste crept into the workshop, moving gingerly among the leaning panes and stacked rods of frozen glass. Each eye, solid, densely cold, fit neatly into the palm of her small hand.

She would light the small gas lamp over her father's workbench and slowly roll the eye in the flickering yellow glow. The milky white of the orb; the glittering blue or green or hazel of the iris, shot through with specks of light and dark; the black target of the pupil. Size, her father had explained, was everything. Too small a pupil would make the customer look shifty, like a criminal. Too large would make them eternally permanently shocked or surprised. Though wider pupils could be attractive in a lady, it was important that both eyes matched. A fraction of a fraction of an inch was all the difference between a normal eye and that of an opium addict.

Sometimes he gave her the eyes that had failed: the orbs too ovoid, or the irises distorted and non-circular, or the pupils doubled-up or misplaced. Glass was a fickle thing. She rolled them like deformed marbles down the wooden floor of the hallway, their different weights and shapes giving each eye its own unique pattern of movement. Even a perfect eye—he had given her one of those, a peculiar but appreciated gift—was not a true sphere, with the little bulge of the cornea disturbing the perfect curve.

Celeste watched her father's customers with fascination. They would visit regularly but infrequently, every couple of years or so. A glass eye, if well-made, might easily last a lifetime, but the socket's shape changes with time, necessitating a new lodger. Often the customers wanted to keep their old eyes, having a sentimental if not a bodily attachment to the little creations, but sometimes they sold them back to their maker, who, if he was lucky, might be able to find them a new home in another skull. One customer, a wealthy fidgeter, came frequently for replacements. He could not resist playing with his eye, taking it out, rolling it round and showing it off, dropping it in his friends' drinks. Soon the eye would be scratched or chipped; would catch the light wrongly, necessitating replacement.

Celeste learned the lore of lost eyes. An eye long dead might be clouded over or rolled back inside the head: an ugly fate, the dead organ best replaced by something glass. The removal was a surgeon's job—a delicate one. Celeste's father explained that, through the back of the eye socket, it was possible to gain direct access to the brain. In a way, the eyes were the brain extruding through the skull into the outside world, seeking in-formation. The brain, he explained, rather than the heart, was the seat of thoughts and emotions, of spirit and soul. The heart was a pump, a machine, nothing more. Celeste's father had wanted to be a surgeon, but had lacked the necessary opportunities. He had studied a little, though, and his knowledge of anatomy was a well of limitless fascination for his eldest child. He loved bodies for both their mechanical perfection and their surprising failures. Often he complimented his wife, Celeste's mother, on the neatness of her musculature, the tidiness of her facial structure. Though he had no time for phrenology, he fostered a secret belief in physiognomy. The tidier, the more symmetrical a person's body, the more Celeste's father liked them. He had no time for the obese or disproportionate, which was why he took such pride in the perfection of the eyes he would make for his customers. He was restoring their symmetry, giving them back their decency. The most painful job he ever had was to make a deliberately mismatched eye for an eccentric farmer, who wanted an iris of gold and a pupil of red. It would keep the stockmen in line, the man had explained, laughing a queer little laugh.

Celeste was like her mother. Symmetrical and neat, she was her father's favourite. Her brother had mismatched ears and refused to centre-part his hair, while little Faith had a small rhinoceros-shaped birthmark on the left side of her face. Celeste's father loved the children dearly, but he was suspicious of their characters.

Celeste grew up within shouting distance of the railway station in Redfern. When her father's customers arrived there, she would be dispatched down the street to fetch them, bringing them to his workshop. Most were men, from all walks of life. Some had impressive scars, from burns or fights. These were usually the least talkative. A glass eye alone would never hide all the damage that misfortune and bravado had done their faces. They were often big men who walked like bears, embarrassed to be seen being led by a small blonde girl. Others were more friendly, making polite, if condescending, conversation with her, and usually seemed happy to answer her probing questions about the fates of their various lost eyes. Usually they talked of accidents, of flying stones or kicking horses, of tools turned to shrapnel in the middle of use. Occasionally they told her about dramatic fights. One man explained his encounter with a hot poker in loving detail, grinning at Celeste's shivers. From these men she learned that a glass eye left in place overnight can cause the head to ache horribly the next morning, and that grit on the eye can irritate the orbits of the skull.

Much less common were the women, and these Celeste pitied. It seemed to her that a man who had lost an eye did not really suffer for it. It was just a thing that had happened to him, the inspiration for jokes, for stories, for a little irritation. Even an ugly man could still be a successful man. Some could even turn their ugliness into a strange charisma. But the women seemed so sad, with their gaping sockets in slender faces, with their walks which showed how aware they were of their defect. An ugly woman could not be a successful woman, and even those who kept their beauty acted as though it had gone with their eyes. They talked much less than some of the men, tended not to linger in her father's workshop. It was brightly lit—this part of Sydney was the first to get electricity, and her father was as enthusiastic about this new technology as he was about everything else that intrigued him—and could be a shock for the self-conscious.

It was at school, through talking to the other girls, that Celeste discovered something strange about her family. Every other girl was named after her father, but her surname was Gibbons, which came from Celeste's mother. At home she asked her father why this was. He referred to "unpleasantness" down south in one of the other colonies, but would tell her nothing more. 'Gibbons' was a safer name to trade under than whatever it was he had abandoned.

On the shelf above the row of eyes, her father kept a row of books. When Celeste was old enough to reach them, she spent hours poring over the massive cloth-bound volumes. *Kirke's Physiology* filled numerous pages with discussions of the human eye. She learned why glass eyes could still move like real ones. If well made, and her father's were always well made, the tightly fitting glass eye could still touch the six ocular muscles. The names of these muscles made a bizarre poetry: *internal rectus, external rectus, superior rectus, inferior rectus, superior oblique, inferior oblique.* Occasionally a glass eye might slip in place, and then be twitched round by these muscles in a fascinating display of misaligned pupils.

When she was fourteen she was taken out of school in order to help her parents around the house. Her father proudly demonstrated the basic principles of glass-blowing, and the similarity of modern glass-blowing equipment to that which had been used since the seventeenth century. He let her work on eyes of her own, for an hour each evening, after she had helped her mother clean up the dinner plates. Her first was a horrible, bloated thing, with a runny iris and oval pupil, but Celeste's father explained that she need not fret—it was a fine first attempt.

That November, two passenger trains collided in Redfern station. The noises of screeching, twisted metal, escaping steam and panicked screams reached Celeste and her father in his workshop up the road. He was working on a blue iris, while she was sweeping all of the tiny fragments of glass out from underneath the benches, trying to stay away from the brutal heat of the furnace.

They both ran down to the station, joining a milling

crowd of confused, shouting people. The first-class carriage of one train had been lifted clear from the rails by the force of the collision and the momentum of the other train. The locomotive, which had been running backwards—a dangerous practice, as the papers later bemoaned—was driven into one of its own carriages, and partially demolished. The other engine, which had been backed into, was an astonishing sight. The boiler had exploded, its erupting pipes broken and unfurled, pointing in dozens of directions, like her father's shaving brush rendered in steel, or some industrialist's nightmare after a meal of spaghetti. The carriages had been filled with scalding steam. Though many of the windows were broken, the iron bars over the shattered glass prevented the passengers from escaping. Celeste saw one man staggering from the wreckage, his forearms denuded by the heat of the steam, his skin hanging down in long, curling, raw strips over his hands like inverted, tattered gloves. But he was more fortunate than the passengers still trapped, who were inhaling the blistering vapour. Choking cries came from the buckled carriages.

Celeste's father helped drag one man clear of the wreckage, the fellow's upper body seared and swollen. He could not breathe, and began to choke and thrash about horribly. With the assistance of a hand-wringing policeman, Celeste's father used his pocket knife to perform a primitive tracheotomy on the gentleman, opening his neck at the throat to allow the passage of air, staunching the flow of hot blood with wads of material torn from the man's sodden shirt.

When the fellow, now breathing but looking worse than ever, was finally taken off on a stretcher, Celeste stood with her father by the side of the platform, streaked with sooty condensation.

"Ah my darling," he sighed, putting a hand around his daughter's shoulders and looking into her wide grey gaze. "What a day! I always knew I had it in me!"

Unsure of how to react, she held his long-fingered hand and gazed into the wreckage.

"Perhaps some of them'll need new eyes?" she piped. He laughed and ruffled her hair.

"Aye, well, you never know your luck, darling," he grinned.

The Mermaid of Brisbane

In the final week of the century, the Mermaid of Brisbane dived and turned in the cramped limits of her murky tank. The flickering lamplight glittered on her scales as she rolled in the depths, before rising once more. For a moment her pale face broke the surface, bringing gasps from the circle of children and their parents. It was an appreciative audience still suffused with Christmas goodwill. Then she dove again, a trail of silvery bubbles drifting up behind her.

§

"Mother? Mother, you must eat."

Her mother was a little over sixty, but seemed much older, aged by circumstance, insanity, and second-hand clothes. Elizabeth sighed as the older woman pushed the plate of food away across the heavy table. Around them other inmates capered and shuffled, under the imperious gaze of a poorly carved statue of Dymphna, patron saint of the insane.

"Mother!" Elizabeth snapped, frowning. The old woman made a face at her and looked away, affecting deafness. Reluctant to stoop to it, but aware that it was the only thing which would work, Elizabeth began to spoon the lukewarm stew into her own mouth. Immediately her mother grabbed the bowl and began eating.

"Miss Gibbons?" said a voice behind her, soft and Welsh. "A while since we've seen you, eh?"

Elizabeth stood to curtsy to the doctor. "I've been away, Doctor."

The portly gentleman nodded and fiddled with his half-moon spectacles. He wore an expensive but somewhat threadbare waistcoat under a dark jacket, with an ostentatious gold chain attached to a large pocket watch.

"Come, let's take a turn in the grounds."

"Mother," said Elizabeth, turning back to the old woman. "We're going for a walk outside."

In answer, her mother gripped the table and shook her head. Elizabeth sighed again. The doctor smiled.

"When she's in these contrarian moods she will only obey if you request the opposite of what you would have her do. On some washing days we can only get her to dress by attempting to take away her fresh clothing. Or we must say she can only have bread in order to have her eat her meat. Missus Gibbons? You must not follow us, you hear?"

As Elizabeth and the doctor walked away toward the door, they heard Elizabeth's mother moving surreptitiously after them.

"Is there any improvement?" Elizabeth asked, stepping out onto the neatly trimmed lawn. The doctor squinted up at the morning sun and then peered down at his watch.

"I'm afraid not, Miss Gibbons, though we have not abandoned all hope. A strict diet may yet do some good, and we are installing a new water pump in the bath house. There seems evidence that a good, cold hosing can work wonders with even the most recalcitrant, better than the still baths we have now."

Missus Gibbons now walked alongside them, taking her daughter's hand. Her palm was dry and unexpectedly warm. For a moment Elizabeth felt like a child again. Her mother had seemed like a giantess once, before her sickness.

"A lovely day," the old woman remarked, temporarily lucid. "Where's Mary?"

"She lives in Sydney now, Mother. You remember?" Elizabeth said.

"She married that glass-blower?"

"Yes." Elizabeth hadn't seen her sister in years.

"Poor Mary. They took you children away from me, you know."

"No, we took *you* away, Deidre," interrupted the doctor, loudly. Turning back to Elizabeth he grimaced again. "We find it best not to indulge their self-pity."

The three walked on in silence for a few moments, until they were nearly across the lawn. The hospice's grounds were not large, though the building itself was. The whole of the place was surrounded by a high fence of wrought iron, topped with barbs. In its first years of operation there had been some opposition to the asylum from the wealthy families who lived nearby.

"Your father was an officer of the law, was he not? Killed in the line of duty?" asked the doctor. Elizabeth nodded, bored by his ponderousness. "Perhaps if he had not taken such a risky occupation your mother would have found the strength she needed in him."

Elizabeth frowned, but said nothing. Her father had died before she was born, but her mother had never seemed at all weak, until the day she began to complain of the angels talking in her head.

"Gibbons. An interesting name. Welsh origin, I suspect," the doctor continued, apropos of nothing in particular. "From the Gaelic 'gibean,' meaning a hunchback. Was your father Welsh?"

"No, nor hunchbacked. Though I don't know about his own parents. He came over from England in the Fifties. He met my mother on the boat."

"Ah, yes, a great journey at sea can also cause some upset to a female mind. So much can go wrong with a woman." He nodded to himself. "Wombs, you know," he added, gesturing vaguely.

Elizabeth's mother suddenly let go her hand and began wandering off across the grass, toward where an unkempt gentleman in cricketing whites was sitting at the base of a tree. "Your mother seems to have formed an attachment to that fellow," the doctor remarked. "He's an odd one. Claims to be the reincarnation of Mister W. G. Grace. We've told him many a time that the man's not dead, but he'll not listen. Quite mad." He stared off, lost in his thoughts for a moment. "Still, I see no reason to obstruct their friendship, as long as it remains within bounds, so to speak. Come, Miss Gibbons, to my office. We must settle the accounts."

§

Flipping her mermaid's tail, Elizabeth dove to the bottom of the tank. To the audience crowded above she was nothing but a shimmering blur of pale colour. At the bottom she held onto the narrow pipe, pinched the rubber mouthpiece and pulled out the cork before sucking in fresh air. The other end of the pipe was at the top of the tank, hidden under a cloth banner. This way she could maintain the illusion that she did not need to surface for breath. Down in the cold water she could hear the steady booming of a child's foot, kicking idly against the outside of the tank.

She pushed off the bottom with her constrained legs and rose toward the light one last time, trying to maintain what Patrick called her "nymph's smile." Then, just before breaking the surface, she arched her back and sank again, distantly hearing the gasps of delight.

Crouched at the bottom of the tank, she breathed air again and waited for Patrick to clear out the audience. Looking up, she saw one of the lamps go out, her signal that it was safe. She bobbed up into the tent's sawdust-scented air.

"Look at this!" Patrick grinned at her, showing the pile of coins in his hat. Elizabeth hauled herself up onto the edge of the tank and then slithered over, landing awkwardly on her "tail." She was naked aside from the green silk wrapped tightly around her hips and legs, knotted at the feet so as to produce two fin-like shapes, reinforced with triangles of wire. Shivering, she pulled the silk free and hung it over the side of the tank before reaching for her threadbare towel. Patrick was counting aloud.

"Two quid clear profit this week!" he laughed, capering on the spot. "I can't remember when it was last as good as this!"

Elizabeth covered herself as much as the towel would allow, checked that the tent's flaps were tied shut, then began to wring out the silk of her tail.

"Oh, me darling!" Patrick grinned, wrapping up the money in a handkerchief and shoving it into his trouser pocket. He came over and kissed her, sliding one hand up under the towel and between her thighs. She inhaled deeply, then gave a sudden yelp as something cold and hard intruded. Patrick backed away, grinning. Elizabeth reached down and removed a shilling piece.

"I'm taking you to dinner, my mermaid!"

§

She and Patrick had been to Sydney once, to that teeming, noisy, dirty place of half a million, and now she dreamed of it often. They had worked for three months as part of a sideshow. In the mornings Elizabeth had watched the mist rise from the Blue Mountains in the west, replaced each day by the oily vapour of the gumtrees that scattered the light and gave the range its vivid colour. She had worked in the company of freaks: a bearded woman, a man covered in tattoos of dragons and angels, and an Irish giant almost twice her height who read and re-read Fanny Burney to pass the time.

The disturbing, strangely erotic air of the sideshow had stayed with her. The tattooed man had paraded near-naked, displaying his ink-stained flesh. More than one man had propositioned her, though many had also propositioned the bearded lady.

Brisbane was a jumped-up country town by comparison, but one where she and Patrick managed to turn a steady trade each summer. They set up in the south, near the banks of the river, where water for the mermaid tank did not need to be carried far. Memories were still strong here of the 1893 flood, when the city's main streets were underwater, half of the Victoria Bridge was swept away, and three-dozen lives were lost. Seven years on, and water still inspired fear and fascination in those who continued to live at its mercy, and a half-glimpsed mermaid who lived in that element drew the crowds.

For the rest of the year they travelled up the coast

and back. Through Sandgate and Maryborough; through Bundaberg, where frangipani trees lightened the banks of the Burnett River; through Gladstone, where they set up by the sea to catch the families on warm coastal days; through Rockhampton, where Patrick had made friends among the Chinese, from whom he learned unlikely bits of lore concerning "dragon lines" which he used to expand the mysticism of his patter. In bad years they went as far afield as Mackay, hundreds of miles north, in search of an audience with pennies to spare for the show. In every town they bolted together the tank, stuffing the holes and gaps with tightly twisted hessian, and then Patrick would roam the streets putting up their posters. She liked being in the north, in places where there were stretches of river or coast where she could swim naked, completely alone, for hours. She would dive as deep as she could for as long as she could. The only sounds she could hear were the slow release of breath and the thumping of her heart.

In the end they always returned to Brisbane, where Elizabeth had been born.

Her father had been a sergeant in the Native Mounted Police, taking squads of blacks into the scrub to hunt down other blacks. He'd been killed by one of his own men, three months before Elizabeth had been born, and from what Elizabeth's mother had let slip it was a surprise it had not happened earlier.

Now her mother was in an asylum, and her siblings had scattered. Patrick was the only person Elizabeth felt close to. She sometimes believed she loved him, but she would not marry him. She was determined not to gift her mother's insanity to the future.

§

She woke late morning, alone on the last morning of the century, from dreams of hammering shut a packing case that was leaking copious amounts of blood. Patrick had set off the previous afternoon, allegedly to settle their debts with the printer and the banks, but he was probably on a bender. Elizabeth lay awhile in the curtained gloom, letting the dream dissolve, listening to the sounds of life outside. The Colony of Queensland would cease at midnight. The State of Queensland, of the new Commonwealth of Australia, would be born in its place.

Elizabeth arose slowly, stretching her legs before swinging her feet to the cool boards of the floor. From somewhere below she could smell the brothy kitchen odours as the landlady prepared an early lunch for those lodgers who had paid the extra. The sunlight which leaked through the curtains dappled a poster for the Paris Olympics that Patrick had torn from the newspaper and pinned to the wall.

She stood in front of the fly-specked mirror at the foot of the bed. How many more years could she play the mermaid, she wondered. How many more years before the mermaid's body betrayed her, before it could no longer earn its keep? She remembered the others she had known at sideshows through the years, the dancers and acrobats who lost their flexibility and grace, who couldn't take a tumble without the risk of shattered hips. The old fortune-teller who could no longer remember what her cards meant. Only the bearded lady had prospered, becoming bushier and more wiry by the month.

Elizabeth dressed and steered her thoughts away

from Patrick's whereabouts. She put the money he had thrown at her into a purse and concealed it inside her dress. Then she went downstairs and out into the noisy street.

§

When Elizabeth saw the small crowd standing by the tent, she at first took them for customers.

"No show today," she said, coming up to them. "I'm sorry. No show today."

The five or six gawkers moved out of her way, letting her see the damage. Somebody had hacked at the tent with a knife, leaving strips of it to hang down like flaps of peeling bark. Going inside, she saw that the tank had been battered so violently that it was quite out of shape, huge gaps showing at the distended seams. The green silk of her tail had been shredded and left in tatters scattered over the trampled grass. A foot had been put through the face of the mermaid on the sandwich-board Patrick had made up and sometimes wore. Obviously he had not settled their debts to everybody's satisfaction.

"Well," she said, quietly, surveying the damage. One of the gawkers had come in behind her, and he looked around with interest.

"Gave the place a right going over," he said, in the cheery tones of somebody for whom it was not his problem. "Dear oh dear."

"Excuse me," Elizabeth said. She picked up a piece of the torn silk and then pushed past him.

She hired a cab to take her over the river and into Hamilton, the higher ground where the wealthy families had moved after the flood. The day was now quite warm, and she was sweating as she climbed the slope towards the asylum gates. The doctor answered himself when she knocked.

"Ah, Miss Gibbons! How unexpected to see you again so soon. I thought you might have gone up-country again."

He led her to his office, ignoring the ape-like whooping which came from somewhere in the asylum. Each time she came here it seemed even more crowded with books. Many of them were non-medical, the doctor having an obvious fascination for scientific romances and tales involving pirates and brigands. An open copy of some novel with a luridly rendered skull on the cover was face-down on his desk, partially obscuring a chart covered with sketches of brains. He went to hide it, then changed his mind and showed it to her. "Blood and thunder stuff. Quite silly. But how I love it!" He gave a childlike smile.

"I keep meaning to join a library, but we never stay put long enough to make it worth the cost," Elizabeth said.

"Oh, you must!" the doctor cried. "There's nothing like losing yourself in nonsense!"

"Presumably as long as you don't get so lost as to end up an inmate here?"

He laughed uproariously. "Exactly so! Exactly so! Very good. So, what might I do for you? You were only here the other day," asked the doctor.

"I would like to spend tomorrow with my mother," Elizabeth stated. The doctor pursed his lips.

"Ah," he said. "Impossible, I'm afraid. The asylum will be closed to visitors up until Wednesday morning, you see. The Federation celebrations."

Elizabeth withdrew the purse from her dress and tipped its contents out onto the desk.

"I would like to spend tomorrow with my mother," she repeated, quietly.

The doctor gave her a long, searching look. Then he reached over and pushed the money back toward her.

"If you promise to bring her back first thing the next morning, then you can take your mother out tomorrow."

Elizabeth looked startled. "Out of the hospital grounds?"

"I don't see why not. She is not a danger to herself or others. The angels may talk to her, but they don't direct her to harm. If you keep a steady hand on her shoulder then I can't see any difficulties arising. A change of scenery might even do her some good."

Elizabeth looked down at the money and then back up at the doctor. "You don't want to be paid for it?" she asked.

"I am not a villain, Miss Gibbons. Dear girl, tell me, is that your best dress?"

This unexpected question took her off-guard. "Yes," she said.

"Perhaps that money might be better spent on a new frock. A woman should always try to be beautiful, Miss Gibbons. Good for the character, which is good for the mind."

She hesitated in her seat, then rose, scooping the money into her hands once more. The doctor gave her a sad, kind smile and opened the door for her.

"Please be here at eight in the morning to fetch your mother," he said.

§

The mermaid and her mad mother took an omnibus into town for the celebrations.

"Horses don't like people," the elder lady remarked. "They can smell the meat on our breath."

The omnibus windows were thrown open, the fresh breeze pleasant on the faces of mother and daughter. The clear blue sky promised heat again, and the passengers had dressed appropriately—the men in cool flannels and silks, the women in diaphanous muslins or thin jackets. Outside, scarlet sunshades hung below the familiar green of the palm trees. Each veranda they passed was decorated with ribbons and flags, and as they neared the centre of the city they saw that the streets were already filling with smiling revellers. Newspaper boys were selling commemorative supplements. "Once in a lifetime!" one bawled, over and over.

They descended to the footpath several blocks from Queen Street and walked the rest of the way, as the roads were too choked with pedestrians for the omnibus to take them any further. "Have you ever seen anything like it, Mother?" asked Elizabeth, looking around in awe. It seemed to her as though every citizen of the city must have come out to celebrate. Every balcony overlooking the streets had become a box-seat. Women leaned over the rails, fans in their hands, and waved to those below. Several children, dressed in their Sunday best, threw great fistfuls of confetti down from a second-storey window. "Crowds are dangerous," Elizabeth's mother frowned. "Contagious disease, my dear. They've the plague in Sydney, you know. We could all sicken and die."

"There's no plague here, mother."

On Queen Street there was barely space for them to

fit, let alone move or breathe. Elizabeth held her mother close, whispering calming words to disarm the old woman's worries about assassins and pickpockets. The crowd was densest in front of the Treasury Building, where the Governor was to give his speech. A few daring souls had secured themselves the best view by scaling the building's parapets. They walked heel-toe-heel-toe above the heads of the mob, grinning at their own bravery.

"Do you think there will be fireworks? I loved fireworks when I was a girl."

"There'll be fireworks, Mum. As soon as it's dark."

Somebody had set church bells ringing. The noise was joined by the shriek of steam-whistles from the direction of the river. Elizabeth's mother gave a start, and began muttering darkly to herself about the power of sudden frights to stop the heart. "Turns it to stone," she said, nodding sagely. "Terrible business." She squeezed her daughter's hand. "Thank you, dear."

"That's all right, Mum."

And so ensued what was for Elizabeth the cheerful boredom of it all: the Governor, the dignitaries and their immaculate wives, the speeches, the Queen's proclamation, the uniting of the new nation, the telegram from the Secretary of State for the Colonies to welcome Australia to her place among the nations. The prayer and the "Amen!", the crowd's wild applause. Elizabeth smiled at the joyous sound and at her mother's look of babyish awe. And then, as a choir of three-hundred children began to sing "God Save The Queen," she watched the old woman's face change to one of simple, deep happiness.

"The beautiful children!" she murmured, eyes half-closed as she listened. "Oh, listen to the angels!" Her grip on Elizabeth's hand grew even tighter, and her daughter leaned into her. Flowers were thrown down from the balcony above, filling the air with petals and perfume.

The Bullet

Imagine the bullet. Very slightly deformed at its base from the cordite explosion which propelled it from the barrel of the rifle, it goes upwards into the air at an acute angle from the vertical, initially moving at more than twice the speed of sound. Millions like it have been used over the last four years, most of them pounded into flesh or brick or wood or earth, but some, too, like this, have been sent heavenward with no lethal intent, in anger or boredom or, as in this case, celebration.

The bullet rises rapidly. Despite the slight irregularity in shape imparted in its firing, it doesn't tumble, though it does rotate around its central axis from the rifling of the Lee-Enfield barrel that sent it on its way.

It's a foggy late morning, the moisture adding to the resistance in the air, slowing the bullet until it breaks free of the fog layer and into clearer air, and the drag reduces. The air, too, is vibrating from the sound of the church bells, though not enough to unduly trouble the bullet's passage. But entropy is inexorable, and gravity too cannot be argued with, and the bullet loses speed as it climbs.

It still climbs a long way, however.

Though he's using a gun borrowed from an English friend, the man who fired it is American. He thinks in terms of feet and inches. But this is Paris, so let's be metric. The bullet rises to a height of a little under two and a half kilometres, reaching its apex south-south-west of its starting point. The first flying humans—Francois Pilatrê de Rozier and Francois Laurent,

Marquis of Arlanders—passed near here, one hundred and thirty-five years earlier, though they attained a mere one-fifteenth of the bullet's maximum height in their Montgolfier balloon. Of course, neither balloon nor bullet can compare with the elevations attained by the fighter planes which have scattered through French skies in the last few years, full of bullets of their own, but then this isn't a competition.

Imagine the fraction of a second when the bullet reaches its apex, when it hangs for an instant, immobile, when the pull of gravity has just extinguished the last of the velocity imparted by the gun fired by Bugler First Class Gordon Harrison of Cincinnati. From this point you can see so much of Paris stretching out below, or you could if it weren't for the fog which makes everything a patchwork of vague grey and blue and brown. The only thing you could clearly make out at this moment is the top of the Eiffel Tower, rising out of the fog to the north-west. The blurry green areas to your east and west, the Bois de Boulogne and the Bois de Vincennes, look from here to be seething under the fog. This is the effect of numerous people congregating to celebrate in the open air.

But ignore those larger open spaces, because from our imagined viewpoint, the place where the bullet hangs for an infinitesimal moment, we should be turning our attention to the greenery of the smaller Jardin des Plantes. This botanical garden is in the 5th arrondissement, on the left bank of the Seine. It is towards a patch of ground here, a little outside the Galerie de Paléontologie et d'Anatomie comparée, that the bullet now moves, gently flipping over to be oriented tip-downwards.

It travels relatively slowly at first, but accelerates quickly, at a little under 9.8 metres per second squared. The moist air once again acts to slightly retard this acceleration, but not enough to avoid the calamity to come. The bullet is only ten grams of metal, but by the time it reaches its terminal point, at the height above ground level of exactly one specific man's head, it will be travelling at something approaching two hundred and seventy kilometres an hour, or a brisk seventy-four metres per second. This, plus its elegant design which tapers to a fine point, concentrates the force it has amassed quite effectively.

The tip meets the skin just above the man's parietal bone, suffering very little resistance from the man's thinning, middle-aged hair. The bullet burrows in, neatly at first, but then with increasingly chaotic effects. Bits of matter that have never seen sunlight are suddenly exposed. The man himself feels no pain, not exactly, but instead a strange and melancholy lurch of longing for *something* as neurotransmitters trigger unconventionally and then go quiet.

And so, at a little over a minute after eleven in the morning on Armistice Day, 1918, Corporal Christopher Gibbons of the Australian Corps, who narrowly escaped machine gun fire months earlier at Villers-Bretonneux, slumps to the ground and promptly expires.

Quality of Light

1. "Self-portrait in Darkroom" by Faith Gibbons: One of the photographer's rare self-portraits, and one which undermines the usual faux-objectivity of photography, as we can see the artist's blurred arm reaching forward to manipulate the camera. The bright cone of electric light in which she stands serves to obscure her features through over-illumination, working in contrast to the way the edges of the image, deliberately overexposed, descend into blackness.

Monochrome prints and chemical baths made up her evenings, spending the late hours in a dark room. The only light allowed in there at these times was red; she was used to seeing her bare forearms tinted by this colour, her sleeves rolled back to keep them from the developing solution. Invisible silver turned black under her careful fingers, a negative image of what had been captured on glass by the camera lens. Dark faces, scarred by transparent eyebrows and luminously open mouths full of black teeth, heads topped by explosions of pale hair. A camera trained on the sun recorded nothing but blackness.

She fixed the negatives in sodium hyposulphite. Once they were washed and dried, carefully handled all the while, she would take a piece of treated paper and make a true image from the glass negative, inverting light and shade again. Though the limitations of monochrome offered possibilities, she wished she could use a colour palette. But colour was prohibitively expensive, except on transparencies, and a transparency could not be framed or hung like a print. Still, though lacking in colour, a photograph could be objective and true to what *had* existed, not like words or ink or paint. Of course, there were some tricks of the trade that Faith sometimes used. She indulged in the odd smudging, toning or touching up. The photographs she took of herself were usually without the grey shade of her birthmark.

She preferred to wear a shirt and trousers in the darkroom, though out in the world she usually clothed herself in an inoffensive dress and modest hat. The Great War had changed some things, but Faith could not afford to lose the custom of even the most reactionary people, for whom her sex might be a stumbling block. There was a lot of work, but it did not pay well.

She dreamed of war photography, but the images Faith captured were from another world entirely. Instead of frozen moments of mud and blood, shattered trees and smoke, she had images of happy families, gum trees, and the endless Australian sun.

§

2. "Mrs. Peter West of Kings Cross" by Faith Gibbons: One of the artist's many Snapshots from Home League photographs, though not many are known to have survived—though she kept copies in her archive, most of these were destroyed in the 1952 fire which ruined her then-studio. This photo is unusual in having been taken outside, in the street. The subject

has not been definitively identified.

Her mornings were spent working for the Snapshots from Home League. The Young Men's Christian Association had promised every serviceman a picture from home, delivered to "wherever a horse could go." At half-past eight each morning, Faith reported to one of the Sydney branches for a list of addresses. At each waited wives, children, mothers, fathers, fiancées, girlfriends. The work took her all over the city. On more than one occasion she had dispatched Snapshots from Home to a man who had once sat, a fresh volunteer in his new uniform, sheepish in one of her studio's chairs.

In the early afternoon she would buy a newspaper and read it over lunch in a park or a train station, wondering how much longer the work would last. With the war over, it was only a matter of time. Though tens of thousands of Australians were still stuck in France or the Middle East, or lying in British hospitals, they were slowly being brought back. Faith sometimes thought about those she had captured on glass, like water creatures on a microscope slide. How many had survived? How many of those were now unrecognisable?

§

3. "George Street with 'Stormy' between the shafts" by Faith Gibbons: The busy Sydney street, photographed at midday if the shadows are any guide, is a backdrop to the enormous blinkered Clydesdale which fills much of the frame. Gibbons photographed a number of street scenes, but seems to have been rarely

satisfied with them—few appeared in her later exhibitions. This image is also notable because it inadvertently captures a crime in the act: in the upper left-hand-corner, an unidentifiable small boy can be seen in the act of picking the pockets of a gentleman in a long coat.

Faith moved on, as fast as she was able in her narrow skirt. She was due to take more Snapshots from Home this morning, and would be lucky to get to her appointed subjects before lunch. An enclosed automobile bounced past her. Faith desperately wanted to try driving a car, but she knew nobody who had access to one. How long before the horse vanished from the streets?

§

4. "Mr. Nicholas Fitzgibbon, Dorothy and Joan, at home" by Faith Gibbons: One of a series of photographs Gibbons took of this wealthy Sydney family, and one which shows her eye for the unusual. The oddly positioned mirrors and the hanging fabric, intricately quilted and subdivided into rectangles by the shadow of a set of windows, add a disquieting set of patterns and doubles which introduce a real feeling of unease into what should be a standard family portrait.

"I'm a Fitzgibbon and you, my dear, are a Gibbons. We may be, in some distant way, related." Mister Fitzgibbon was a widower, an Irishman, something of a spiritualist, and the father of five daughters and one son. He was large, talkative and friendly, and had rough, red, flaking skin that reminded Faith of brickwork.

She pushed the curtains of the front room back as far as they would go, so as to let in as much natural light as possible. Fitzgibbon, twin ten-year-old daughters on each side of him, sat against the backdrop of a quilt made by his late wife.

"The 'Fitz' prefix was taken by illegitimate sons sent to make a life for themselves in Ireland or the colonies. Perhaps some forgotten ancestor of yours fathered some bastard ancestor of mine?"

"I doubt any of my ancestors were distinguished enough for such scandals to matter," Faith replied, turning back to look at him. The twins, who had initially been excited at the prospect of being photographed, were now quite bored with the wait.

"Convict stock, eh?"

Faith was unsure whether he considered that possibility a blessing or a curse. "No, not at all. My grandparents came out here of their own free will. My grandfather was a policeman, in fact."

"A policeman, no less. Dear me."

Faith knew very little about spiritualism, and was nonplussed when Nicholas Fitzgibbon began talking of his wife in the present tense.

"We still communicate," he explained. "Fiona, my eldest, is very sensitive to the other side."

Faith had yet to meet Fiona. The girl was sick and in bed. The occasional outburst of ragged coughing from some distant part of the long, narrow house was the only evidence of her existence. As soon as she had taken a photograph of the twins with their father, the girls fled with relief. Fitzgibbon watched them go without comment, a fond look on his face. "Marvellous girls," he said. "I'll just go and find the others, shall I?"

Once he was outside, Faith began to set up for another shot. She heard a voice calling from elsewhere in the house. She hesitated, but Mister Fitzgibbon was still outside rounding up daughters, so she raised her own voice in response.

"Hello?"

"Who's that? Where's Father?"

"Ah, your father's just gone outside for a moment. Can I help?"

There was a pause, and then another cough. "Who *are* you?" the voice called, sounding annoyed.

Faith made sure that her tripod could not be easily upset, and then ventured through a doorway leading into a long corridor. There were half a dozen other doors, mostly open, and the distinct sound of coughing was coming from the farthest away.

When Faith poked her head in, she saw a girl of twenty or so propped up in a large bed. Her wan features and thin hair made her look like a softer, paler version of her father.

"Er, hello? My name is Faith. I'm the photographer your father hired."

"Oh. The photos for my brother?" the girl asked. She looked to have been in bed for quite some time. The bed was covered with a scattering of various open books, magazines, letters, and stained handkerchiefs. Despite the open window, there was a distinct odour of urine from some concealed chamber pot. The girl was holding a pencil, with which she was making marks in the margin of one of the books.

"Your brother? Yes. I'm sorry if I'm disturbing you. Was there anything you wanted?"

"Well, yes, there was, actually. Some water." She indicated an empty china jug that sat on the dressing table. "Please."

As Faith moved forwards to get the jug, Mister Fitzgibbon came into the room.

"Fiona, please, don't be ordering visitors around like that. Excuse me, Miss Gibbons, allow me to do that."

"Oh, it's no trouble..."

"Honestly, no, I couldn't let you!" He took the jug from her and then stood in the doorway, obviously waiting for Faith to follow him out. After glancing back at the girl, who seemed unperturbed, she went after him.

"The other girls are waiting for you," he said, gesturing towards the front of the house. "They're a little better behaved than the twins, so you shouldn't have too much trouble."

"Ah, well. Of course." She nodded, and then paused. "And Fiona? When would you like me to photograph her?"

"Oh. No, I don't think that will be necessary. No. She's dying, you see. We don't want to upset my son, do we?"

§

5. "Celeste" by Faith Gibbons: An unidentified woman, her arms outstretched, caught in movement, blurred like a dancer, her dress thrown outwards by centripetal force. Her face is mostly in shadow, a narrow slice of horizontal light revealing only her dark-

rimmed eyes. The title suggests that this may be the artist's older sister, Celeste.

Faith was surprised by the odd man one afternoon when she was preparing to close for the day. There were no sessions booked, and she wanted to tidy up. Now that the pubs were forced to close at six, every man spent the last hours of the afternoon sinking as much booze as he could in the time allotted. Portraiture was the furthest thing from their thoughts.

He was middle-aged, undistinguished, remarkable only for his mutilated hand. Even as she opened her mouth to welcome him, part of her was thinking of how to rectify the missing digits on a print. Careful smudging while the photo was wet to draw out the shapes of the stumps would do the trick, though it might not look as natural as she would wish.

"Good afternoon, sir," she smiled, throwing away a tiny curtsy. Behind the man stood a woman with short feet and a tall head. She gave the impression of having been made from a rolled tube of paper by a child who wasn't paying attention to proportions. "Ma'am."

The man nodded and smiled awkwardly. He was dressed in an overcoat, with dark trousers protruding from the bottom and red-tipped cuffs from the sleeves. Under one arm he held a military helmet, and under the other a paper-wrapped package.

"You'll be able to sort this out, won't you dear?" asked the woman, nudging her husband's arm. "I've got to get to the hall quick-smart, clean up before them fellas show up." Without waiting for a response, she headed off. The bell over the door tinkled a tired farewell.

"And what might I do for you?" Faith asked. The man

gave a nervous shrug,

"Ah, I'd like a photograph done," he said, his voice suggesting that he expected her to fly into a fury at this imposition on her time. Faith grinned, pleased. The nervous chaps were much easier customers to deal with than the bossy ones, who had their own ideas about how to pose and how best to use a camera.

"Certainly, sir. A uniformed portrait, I see."

The man nodded, jamming his helmet onto his head. Faith took the coat and package from him, setting them down on one chair and then waving a hand at another. "Please," she added, "sit down. I'll just take a few minutes setting everything up."

The man folded himself carefully into the chair, still helmeted. He tucked his damaged hand inside his jacket, which was black and collared with red.

As she worked, Faith began chatting to him, trying to make the man feel more at ease. "You served in the army then?"

"Ah, yes, against the Boers. Eighth Irish Rifles." He smiled briefly up at her, then frowned. "Lost me sword after I got back..."

Faith opened the curtains once more, filling the studio with the remains of the daylight. "Is this portrait for your wife, then?"

"Ah, no... Our son, actually. He's still stuck in France, waiting for a berth home. Thought it might buck him up, you know? Remind him his old dad's been through it too." He sighed and glanced about. "Is your husband over there somewhere?"

Faith shook her head. "I'm not married," she explained, not looking out from under the hood, where she was carefully inserting a plate into the camera.

"Oh, I'm sorry. I just assumed... well, this business, I thought you'd taken over from... well, a woman photographer, eh? You know what I mean?"

She glanced up and smiled, trying to defuse his discomfort. "Don't worry, I'll take a fine picture. Right, would you like to come over here, Sir? Let's arrange you, eh?"

The man got up and, after giving the parcel a nervous glance, came over. She stood him in front of the painted backdrop cloth pinned to the studio wall. He stood stiffly, hands behind his back.

"All changed a bit since my day," he remarked, looking at the camera. "Them things used to be enormous. Huge flash-pans and the like."

"Would you like to be sitting or standing?"

"Oh, ah, standing, perhaps," said the man, shuffling. Faith gave him a smile and nodded. Reading her thoughts, he kept talking. "Me hand, you see. Rather have it out of the picture, eh?"

Faith ducked beneath the hood of the camera again, squinting at her subject. "Look up a little, Sir... That's good. Just hold that pose a moment."

He froze, a statue bathed in the quick splash of light as his image was captured. "Lovely," cooed Faith, straightening up. The man smiled weakly, and relaxed. Faith went over to the small counter in the corner of the room to open her records book. She felt his eyes on her birthmark, just as hers had peered at his hand.

"Do you live nearby?" she asked.

"Ah, yes, just over Manly way."

"Well, if you'd like to come in next week the picture will be ready for you. If you'd just like to give me your details. You'll not be wanting it mounted, I should imagine, not if you're sending it in the post."

The man came over to the counter, his arms jerking oddly as though he had half a mind to flee the building.

"Ah, no," he said, hesitating. Then, suddenly, he lunged at the parcel he had brought and hugged it to him. His helmet was now askew, giving him a comical look. He looked around, then went over to the entrance and began pulling the curtains closed. He turned to look at her, somewhat wild-eyed. "Ah, do you mind if I lock the door, so nobody walks in on us?"

Faith frowned, thinking of the nightstick her father had insisted she keep under the counter in case of difficult customers. "I'm not sure what...," she began. The man gave a wild laugh and then slumped.

"Ah, no, oh dear, I'm sorry, I ought to explain myself. I, it's just, well, you see, there's this, ah, other photograph I was wondering whether you might take."

"Mister Smith, I must warn you, I'll not photograph you in a state of undress."

The man froze, then flushed. "No!" he whinnied. "Sorry, good Lord, not what I was trying to... Well, you see... Blow it, this is awkward! Miss, I need your help. Please hear me out."

Faith folded her arms and leant on the counter, nodding for him to continue. The man turned an even deeper shade of red, and licked his lips despairingly.

"Well, ah, you see, I have this... There's a get-up I like to wear sometimes, you know? But it's so hard, what with the wife. She hates it, it's caused no end of trouble. That's how I lost my fingers, you see? Not by my wife! No, oh dear. In the war. The last war, against the Boers. Not in battle, I mean. You see, I lost them in South Africa, but it was *our* boys that did it to me, do you see?

Frightful business. Didn't like a chap to dress up like that, 'specially not in the army. Not that I had expected anyone to see me. But, well... They weren't just trying to cut off me fingers, you see? I just had my hands in the way, trying to protect myself, d'you understand?"

Faith gaped. The man sighed and began tearing at the parcel, unwrapping a neatly folded length of material. He shook it out, revealing it to be a blue dress, years out of date, and a white petticoat. His eyes were red now, and glittering with tears.

"Please don't judge me harsh, Miss Gibbons. I won't trouble you again if you say no, I understand. Oh Lord this is hard! I just, well, I feel that if I had a photograph to look at sometimes, you know, me being beautiful and so on... You know, if I had the photo I could look at it and not have to *do it*, do you see?"

He took a short step towards her, holding out the unfurled dress. Faith hesitated, then locked the door.

"You'll want some powder," she said. "A little make-up."

§

6. "Siblings" by Faith Gibbons: Two teenaged boys and a teenaged girl, believed to be the children of the artist's younger brother, Iain Gibbons. The poster behind them was included in the archive donated to the National Library after the artist's suicide. It reads, "The fifteen points of a good horse: a good horse sholde have three propyrtees of a man, three of a woman, three of a fox, three of a hare, and three of an asse. Of a man:

bolde, prowde and hardye. Of a woman: fayre-
breasted, fair of haire, and easy to move. Of
a foxe: a fair taylle, short eers, with good
trotte. Of a hare: a grate eye, a dry head,
and well runynge. Of an asse: a bygge chynn, a
flat legge, and a good hoof." That it is the
same poster as that in the photograph is
confirmed by the detail that someone with a
pencil has turned one of the 'm's into a pair
of buttocks with a puff of wind emerging from
between them.

Faith's brother, Marxist and professional gambler, gave a nod. His children scattered with relief, abandoning their stiff poses.

"You won't get them to stay still any longer," he said, smiling indulgently at his sister. "I admire your patience with them."

"It's easy when they're not your own," Faith remarked. "The mothers that come to the studio always look so worn. I can't remember if it was like that before the war. I suspect it was, though."

Iain Gibbons shrugged. "Not everything's set in stone, you know," he said.

Faith began to fold up her tripod. "Politics again?"

"Of course. Always. Everything!" Iain smiled despite himself. He was serious about his beliefs, but it had not escaped him that the fervour of his opinions was a source of amusement to most of his friends and relatives. Since childhood, he had always been the odd one out, and this in a family where one daughter had chosen to carry on their disreputable father's business as a glass-blower and the other daughter had become a photographer. But it was Iain who had married a foreigner—a Croat who had insisted on calling their sons Matej and Petar. It was Iain who had joined the Industrial Workers of the World, the "Wobblies," and who had spent his nights slapping up anti-war posters on Sydney's walls. That night he was planning to take his sons to a lecture on the Russian Revolution by one of the revolutionaries, though on the way he intended to pick up his winnings from a well-placed bet on an amateur steeplechase the previous day. Randwick racecourse was his second home.

"Are you able to come by the studio soon?" Faith asked. "I can have the print ready by tomorrow night, if you like."

"Thank you, that would be perfect." Iain glanced towards where the back door of his house hung open. His children had gone inside. "Listen, there's likely to be a bit of trouble soon, between the Wobblies and the coppers. I might have to vanish for a little bit, until things calm down." He seemed to be relishing the idea. "A picture of the kids will help keep me sane."

"Too late for that."

§

7. "Fiona" by Faith Gibbons: A young woman lies in a bed, propped up by cushions. Her eyes and her mouth are half-open; she looks drawn and thoroughly exhausted. One arm is outstretched along the covers, an open and face-down copy of "Three Men in a Boat" beneath her fingertips is the most obvious of a number of books scattered around the bed.

Everything in the photograph is still.

Having taken the photograph, Faith closed her eyes for a moment and offered a clumsy prayer, the first she had said in a dozen years. Then she turned away from the silent bed and went to the door.

"Mister Fitzgibbon?" she called. "It's done."

The Irishman came in. "I just wanted to make sure," he said. "You never know."

"Honestly, Mister Fitzgibbon, I don't know that... There may well be nothing."

He was sitting on the edge of his dead daughter's bed now, one big paw covering the outflung hand and most of the book.

"I've *seen* them, Miss Gibbons. Spirits in the pictures that were invisible to the people who took them. And Fiona assured me. She *knew things*, you understand?" He looked down at her hand, at the book. "This was making her laugh right up until the end, you know."

Faith hesitated, then went forward to touch his shoulder.

"I just want you to be prepared, just in case... there might be nothing," she repeated helplessly. He had come to her that morning, bursting into her studio with the news that his daughter was about to die, demanding that Faith be there to take a photograph just after the event. When they had arrived, after a strained trip in the taxi, Fiona had welcomed Faith's presence and her camera with equanimity. It had all been her idea, she explained.

"She was my daughter," Fitzgibbon said, his voice breaking with tears for the first time. "I just want to see her soul going safely on its way. It will show in the picture. She *said*."

8. "Fiona" by Faith Gibbons: A young woman lies in a bed, propped up by cushions. Her eyes and her mouth are half-open; she looks drawn and thoroughly exhausted. One arm is outstretched along the covers, an open and face-down copy of "Three Men in a Boat" beneath her fingertips is the most obvious of a number of books scattered around the bed. From her forehead, a bright cross of white light is ascending.

A moment's hesitation in the red light, and then she rubbed carefully at the developing print with the corner of a sponge. The result was not promising. It took her four tries to fake a soul that would comfort Mister Fitzgibbon's heart.

BROTHERLY LOVE
DICK ROGERS

Ink and Oils

A shuffle of movement in the warm glow of the electric light, the room smelling of sandalwood and the mustiness of an un-aired bed. Two young cousins, one sitting up with the book, the other lying back on the pillow, listening.

"He leads me to the table, and with a master-hand lays my head down on the edge of it, and with the other canting up my petticoat and shift, bares my naked posterior to his blind and furious guide: it forces his way between them, and I feeling pretty sensibly that it was going by the right door, and knocking desperately at the wrong one, I told him of it: 'Pooh,' says he, 'my dear, any port in a storm.'"

The two girls cackled, then went quiet at footsteps on the landing. The book shot under the pillow.

"Sleep, girls, sleep," said Aunt Faith from beyond the door, knowing full well this would buy her only ten minutes of peace.

§

The house looked out over a wide yard bordered by wind-ruffled bluegums. Its back faced the street. It was a big old place, designed to be lived in rather than looked at—two stories under a junk-filled attic, sold up by someone who lost all their money with the collapse of the stock market. The place itself came cheap after all of the furniture had been auctioned off, and its shambolic exterior had discouraged other purchasers. With money borrowed from Jean's brother, and that which Lucija had saved from her work in the bookshop, the two women had taken over the deed.

They had celebrated that night, drinking cheap wine on the bare wooden floor, scuffing the polish with their stockings.

Jean's husband had then been gone a year, having taken off when the general economic disaster really began to bite, once he'd claimed what little money there was in the bank. Having been deserted, she did not make inquiries into having the marriage legally dissolved. Jean had no desire to marry again, and if the bastard ever reappeared she intended to have him up in court for the maintenance money she was owed.

Lucija was a spinster still at thirty. This was a disappointment to her mother, who wanted an enormous flock of grandchildren and had received but one, from Matej, her elder son. Lucija had privately welcomed Jean's desertion, since the husband had been a charmless idiot and it meant that the two cousins could band together to get a house. Though they shared only great-grandparents, they were closer to one another than to any of their actual siblings.

They shared the big house with a number of cats, and the yard with a belligerent old peacock known as The Fat Spiv for his preening self-regard. Their property was in Randwick, at the centre of a rough triangle with its corners in Bondi, Centennial Park, and the quieter end of Oxford Street. The immediate neighbours were, by and large, wealthy people who had managed to hold onto their money despite the general economic collapse. Many held an interest in the local racing, to which Lucija's father was a frequent visitor.

On warm nights, when Jean was at her job behind the bar at the local, Lucija would wander down into the garden and sit among the trees, watching as the sun set over Sydney. The steely grey-blue of the leaves would flash in fire, then fade to black. She would rub a leaf between her palms, intrigued by the powdery and faintly aromatic residue it left on her hands. The Fat Spiv would follow her round, hoping for food, until the louder demands from the cats for the same would summon Lucija indoors.

§

It was in the pub, after closing time, that Jean met the artist. She was unimpressed from the start, though he obviously had enough admiration for himself to make up for any lack on her part.

"I paint, you know," he said as an opening gambit, leaning heavily on the bar with a scuffed leather wallet open in his hands. He didn't fit Jean's conception of an artist, being altogether too healthy in appearance.

"Oh yes," she replied, showing as little interest as she could. "And what'll you be drinking?"

"Hmm, let me see. A good whisky, if you have such a thing."

Jean nodded and reached for the bottle, tipping out a measure with care. The artist, like every other customer still on the premises, had signed in the traveller's book, claiming to be passing through the area, which meant he could stay on the premises and keep drinking after six o'clock, when every local was supposed to head home.

"Thank you. Mmm. Tell me, have you ever posed?"

Jean suppressed a smile. "No," she said. "But I know

a poseur when I see one."

The man affected hurt. "Harsh words," he sighed, sipping his drink and pushing a couple of coins across the bar toward her. His voice sounded both English and upper class, the sort of voice that always got her cousin's back up. Though Lucija was not a full-blown Communist like her brothers and father, she became quickly and extremely truculent when exposed to a posh English accent.

"Are you staying in the hotel?" Jean asked. The man shook his head.

"No, I need more space than you've got here. I've just moved into the area, though—taken a room above the furniture place on the next street, enough space for a studio."

"Willoughby's?"

"That's the one. Good light upstairs."

Jean nodded vaguely. Another customer knocked on the bar for attention, a local who always signed in as a traveller under his father-in-law's name, and she went over to serve him.

"So?" asked the artist, reappearing across from her. She noticed that his suit, like his flashed-about wallet, hinted ostentatiously at both wealth and a kind of affected thoughtlessness. Tiny droplets of coloured paint decorated his expensive cuffs. She could imagine him carefully applying them one by one with a fine brush, charmed by himself.

"So what?" she asked, turning back to him.

"So, would you pose for me?" he asked. "I need a redhead. Sick of painting all these damned blondes. I can pay, you know. There'd be good money in it. Better pay than you get here, I'd imagine."

Jean shrugged. "Perhaps."

The artist gave her a searching look, then drained his glass and gave her another flash of perfectly tended teeth. "Well, my dear, you know where I am. 'Willoughby And Sons.' There's a back way in, through the side gate. Just knock."

She nodded in response, amused. The painter smiled a gambler's smile, and then left the hotel.

§

The bound man struggled in the gloom, ineffectually trying to kick out at me. I hit him once with the cricket bat, a sharp blow to the kneecap, and he fell silent.

"If you know what's good for you, you'll keep your mouth shut," I told him, looming over his prone form. He nodded mutely, obviously scared out of his wits. At last my luck was turning. Once I was gone, when this fellow finally managed to free himself, he would go back to his boss and tell him all about what had happened. Then, I hoped, the Parramatta Push mob would think that it was a member of the Blakely mob who had started coming after them. The two gangs would start tearing one another apart, and I could just stand back and leave them to it.

"I reckon he ought to rough the chap up a bit more," Lucija said, setting down her pen and reading through what she had just written. Jean, who was standing by the window, shook her head.

"No—we don't want to overdo it too early," she responded, musingly. "We want a really nice bit of violence at the end, right? It'll just undermine it if we have him getting too tough so soon."

Lucija frowned. "But look what we had him do to his brother in the first book."

"Yeah, but that was at the *end*, wasn't it? Anyway, his brother was the murderer."

Lucija shrugged and then began massaging her wrist. "We should get a typewriter," she muttered. "We can afford it now."

"You can't write poetry on a machine!" cried Jean, scornfully.

"This isn't bloody poetry, not by a long shot! Anyway, it's easy for you to say! You don't have to scribble away for hour after hour."

"You know my handwriting's illegible."

Lucija threw the pen at her cousin in mock anger. "Very damned convenient!"

"Missed!"

"Pfft. Lord, I spend all my time reading and selling literature, and then all I can actually make is this horrible rubbish."

Jean picked up the pen and gave it back. "Well, we'd best get a move on and produce some more rubbish. We said we'd have him find the next body before we finished today."

"The woman from the stockyards?"

"No, the other one, the whore."

Lucija grinned wolfishly. "That's right. We were going to hang her, weren't we? Geoff always likes it when we hang someone."

§

Geoff Marchant was the most obviously homosexual man Lucija had ever encountered, protected from the usual legal consequences by having influential friends and some documentary evidence of an affair he'd once had with a man who was now a high-ranking detective. When he had worked on the stage he had indulged his own personality to the full until he became something of a foppish caricature of himself. His acting career had been terminated by a nasty fall down a stage trapdoor which had left him with a bad limp. A lame actor might be able to do Richard the Third, but Geoff had little future in the romantic leads he so loved. He sunk his savings into a struggling publisher of gardening almanacs, and turned it into a small but flourishing publishing house of mystery novels. Marchant Murder Books and the cheaply stapled 64-page Marchant Bloody Bargains had quickly found their market in a country starved for crime stories set locally.

Marchant was also an accomplished barker, a talent developed during his thespian years. He went round all of Sydney's book shops and newsagents himself, striking deals to get as many of his company's books as possible into the front windows and onto the eye-level shelves. On one of these journeys, he had come into Lucija's book shop.

Lucija had bought the business from the widow of her former employer, a good-natured man who'd been kicked in the head by a horse on George Street. She had continued his trade selling, under the counter, books which had been banned from Australia. The shop managed steady sales of Boccaccio, Balzac, Joyce, Asterley, Huxley, Lindsay, and Lawrence.

On Geoff's second expedition to her shop, Lucija had shown him the manuscript she had written with her cousin. Taking it home, he had read through the night and then returned the next day with an offer of publication. His only condition was that, since the book was written from the first-person perspective of grimy Dick Rogers, it would sell best if published under that pseudonym. The mystery-hungry public, Geoff asserted, would love the fact that it might all just happen to be true. He had been right, though the book's cause had not been harmed by Lucija's shameless promotion of the novel in her own shop. "A brilliant new talent," she told prospective customers, thrusting *Brotherly Love* into their hands. "The real stuff."

Though the success of this book, and its first sequel, was significant, Lucija and Jean had kept up their jobs at the shop and the pub. A thinly populated country like Australia was never going to provide riches through royalties, especially split two ways.

Marchant was a generous man, though, and liked to take the cousins out to expensive lunches or to daring theatrical shows. He had a slumdweller's knowledge of Sydney's underbelly, of the places that felt dangerous and illicit, but which were really fairly safe. In his company they had met a parade of eccentrics and exotics, most of whom, in some form or other, went into the books.

§

The gate squealed on its hinges, sending a dog in the next garden into apoplectic rage. Jean ignored it and went through to the shabby yard behind the furniture shop. The screen door was closed but the back door itself stood open. She went in and stood at the base of the stairs, knocking loudly on the bannister. The place smelled strongly of furniture polish from the shop at the front

"Hello?" she called out.

There was a clatter from above, and then the artist appeared, peering down at her.

"Well, well," he said, looking amused. "I didn't think you'd come. Thought I'd been brushed off."

Jean raised an eyebrow. "It's not too late for that, you know," she remarked. The man grinned and then motioned at her to come up.

"The studio is this way," he said. "Follow me."

There were large windows in the east and west walls, ideal for catching the morning and afternoon sun. A dirty skylight overhead added to the room's warmth. A poseable mannequin of wooden body parts wired together slouched miserably in the corner, a huge and old-fashioned ladies hat tipped forward on its head. A roll of canvas sat near the door, while a few small bits were tacked out onto wooden frames. A larger canvas was on an easel in the centre of the room. Whatever was in the middle of being painted was not immediately identifiable, a dirty wash of brown and grey. Some finished paintings were pinned to the wall over a small bed. A couple seemed to be rudimentary nudes, while the others were mostly primitive landscapes. One very long shelf was bowed under the weight of a number of well-thumbed novels.

"My kingdom," said the artist, bowing to her. "Just let me get sorted out."

As Jean wandered about, examining the books and the mannequin, he took the unfinished picture from the easel and set up a fresh bit of canvas.

"It's a bit cramped, but the light's good," the artist

explained. "What's your name, incidentally?"

"Jean Gibbons," she replied, reaching out to take the mannequin's hand. It had a complete set of delicately tapered fingers, cunningly wired up to mimic the joints and movement of a real human hand.

"Well, Jean, my name's Toby Simpkins. I'm afraid I don't have a screen, love, but that doesn't really matter, does it? If you could just undress, we'll get started."

He gave her a searching look as he said this, obviously expecting her to be shocked, and prepared to be amused at her reaction. Instead, Jean began to disrobe with a stately lack of haste. Simpkins did his best to look equally unimpressed, busying himself with tubes of paint. "Best if you could stand over there," he suggested, once she was undressed. "Under the skylight."

Jean stood in front of him, arms crossed under her breasts, watching as he hummed and hawed over his paint and brushes. His worldly air was starting to evaporate a little in the face of her calm nakedness.

"Ah, very good, very good," he muttered. "If you could just turn a little left... yes, ah, very good. You know, I've been looking for a good redhead model for an age."

He fell silent after a while, making the first marks on his canvas. Jean watched him without moving or talking. It was warm under the skylight, and she felt unusually calm with nothing more required of her than immobility.

"So, Jean," began Simpkins, after almost half an hour of silence. "Any sweethearts?"

"I'm married," she replied, shortly. "Married and abandoned."

The artist blinked in surprise. "Gosh," he said. "And here I was thinking all you colonial girls were innocent and demure."

She laughed and abandoned her pose, going over to the shelf and pulling one of the books from it. The artist watched her as she came back over to him, holding the book out. He took it tentatively—it was *Brotherly Love* by Dick Rogers.

"What's all this about then?" he asked. Jean gave an amused snort.

"I wrote that," she replied. "My cousin, she and I wrote it. We're Dick Rogers. There's another that's been published, and we're writing a third."

The artist squinted at her. The book had been in the room when he'd taken it, and he'd read it soon afterwards. His memories of the plot were full of beatings and not particularly discreet sex. "You're pulling my leg," he muttered. Jean shrugged. Simpkins rubbed his forehead, then set the book down on the easel, a peculiar look on his face. He reached out and, almost tentatively, touched his forefinger to Jean's left nipple. She stared at him. They remained frozen like that for a while and, though she was the one completely naked, Simpkins began to feel deeply ridiculous. He let his hand drop and assumed a sheepish expression.

"Well, best get on before the light moves too much, what-ho?" he mumbled, picking up his brush and making a determined stab at the canvas. Jean went back and assumed her pose. What she'd seen of his painting was not promising.

§

Marchant had called into the shop to take Lucija to lunch. He loitered among the shelves, leafing through an expensive art book of poorly reproduced Renaissance masterpieces, while she sold *Haxby's Circus* to a pale man in a coat covered with cat hair.

"Say, my dear, did you ever hear of a chap named Alphonse Allais?" Marchant asked, once the customer had left. "Froggy gentleman, a painter in the 'nineties." He rapped his knuckles against the cover of the book he had been inspecting. "Exhibited an all-white canvas titled 'Anaemic Young Girls Going to their First Communion through a Blizzard,' an all-black one called 'Negroes Fighting in a Cave by Night,' and an all-red one named 'Apoplectic Cardinals Harvesting Tomatoes by the Red Sea.' Rather amusing." He flicked the book open once more and shook his head over a dark, smudged impression of a mournful face. "More fun than this old nonsense, at any rate."

Lucija laughed and then got up, preparing to lock up the shop.

"How's my book coming?" he asked, flipping his hat onto his head with a dramatic gesture.

"We're still working on it," she replied, smoothing down her dress.

"Hmm. Anything *naughty* in this one?"

She laughed. "A little fornication, perhaps. A girl under the age of consent, though we don't explicitly point that out. A sprinkling of other filth."

Marchant was grinning at her. "What?" she asked.

"I fear the esteemed Dick Rogers is soon to receive the dubious honour of being banned in both Victoria *and* Tasmania."

Lucija scowled. "What are you talking about, Geoffrey?"

"Well, my dear, a little bird of mine south of the

border informs me that they're about to make the advertising of, ah, *contraceptive* devices illegal. Some books will be collateral damage in this little venture. That includes a certain scene with a dutch cap in *Brotherly Love*, if I'm not mistaken."

Lucija was infuriated. "What rot!" she shouted. "That's the most ridiculous thing I've ever heard."

Geoff shrugged. "Lucy, you know they can't ban the importation of our books since they're published here. The puritans have just changed their tactics, I'm afraid."

"Can't you do anything about this?"

He smiled. "Why, I shall be kicking up the most frightfully noisy stink, my dear, and writing to all of the newspapers with a useful checklist of all my titles that could possibly be affected. After all, the vast majority of prudes, I have found, like to get a good look at what enrages them. When something *naughty* goes up in the Art Gallery, the biggest crowds gathered around it are always the clucking conservatives. I don't think you need to fear poverty quite yet, Lucija dear. And you might like to take out some advertisements in the Melbourne and Hobart dailies, noting you can send books by post."

§

Only Jean was at home the next time Lucija's father came to visit. He'd brought his grandson, Lucija's nephew Edgar, who was dressed in odd clothes and wearing a very old hat that was too big for him.

"The only way I could make him come with me to the track was by telling him Ned Kelly had lots of horses," Iain Gibbons explained. "The boy's obsessed with bushrangers."

Jean squatted down in front of the little boy, who was only eight or nine. "And who are you?" she asked, smiling.

"Ben Hall!" replied Edgar, aggravated at yet another person who could not identify him at once. "He never killed anybody, but the police still shot him dead. Thirty bullets dead."

"Poor man," said Jean. "Is Ben Hall your favourite?"

Edgar nodded vigorously, and then shyly produced a detailed cap gun for Jean's inspection. Thanking him, she took it and pretended to fire at the boy's grandfather. Edgar cackled with delight at this cheekiness.

"And *that* is why I'm not going to buy him an air gun," Iain muttered. "Little beggar would shoot me in my sleep."

Smiling, Jean gave back the gun. "Do you like Ned Kelly?" she asked. The boy grinned, his blue eyes bright.

"Ned Kelly had the armour," he said, holstering his gun. "Joe Byrne an' Dan Kelly an' Steve Hart were his gang. They all had the armour. They shot Aaron Sherritt 'cos he told on them to the police and they thought he was their friend."

Iain crouched down alongside Jean, looking into the boy's serious face. "You know why they hanged Ned Kelly, boy?"

Edgar gaped at the stupidity of this question. "He was a bushranger! That's what they *do*!"

Iain shook his head. From the window came the *tap-tap-tap of* The Fat Spiv pecking at his reflection. "Not only that. They hanged him because he was Irish and a revolutionary. He didn't do what the government and the Queen said he should do. He was a free-thinker, was Kelly."

"And a murderer, Uncle Iain," Jean said, straightening up and smiling. "Not everything is political, you know."

Iain laughed. "Oh, never say that. Anyway, you can't blame a man for trying. Got to get 'em when they're young, eh?"

§

I had learned at a young age that one sometimes had to be cruel to be kind. To such a wench as this, one had to be very cruel indeed.

"I could have the police arrest you, Sheila. All your feminine wiles wouldn't stop them charging you with the theft of that money," I explained, looming over her. She was sprawled on the bed still, clothes in disarray, her face red with anger and exertion.

"You're a monster," she announced, slowly. "I hate you, Dick."

I shook my head. "Flattery will get you nowhere, Sheila. Tell me where he is, or you're in for it."

She sat up, letting her dress slide down over a slender shoulder. Her eyes held mine, fierce and passionate.

"I've something else you might be interested in," she said, unsmiling. "How much am I really worth to you, Dick? How much?" I shoved her back down onto the bed.

"You're too old for these games, Sheila," I sneered. "Ten years ago, perhaps it might have worked. Now—well, there are a thousand Sydney girls more than qualified to take your place."

Her only response was a slow, nasty smile. I was already turning when the unmistakable click of a revolver being cocked came from behind me.

69

"That's no way to talk to a lady, Mister Rogers."

I balled my fists, cursing my own stupidity for falling into this trap. "That's no lady, Mister Black," I replied.

§

The seduction, when it came, was not initiated by the artist. Indeed, it was his determination to win her by his charm which had so long delayed Jean from acquiescing to his desires. Only when his spirit and self-confidence were broken did she move on him. She stripped him under the skylight and took him to the low bed under the drying oil paintings. Afterwards, in a post-coital drowse full of cigarette smoke and the lazy sound of a bee which had found its way into the studio, Jean regarded the several paintings she had modelled for. If, like the paintings, the quality of the fucking failed to improve, she didn't have a lot to look forward to.

§

The policeman had the most enormous pair of muttonchop sideburns sprouting from his face, so extensive that Lucija wondered if he was growing them for a bet. He had been waiting on the doorstep of Lucija's bookshop when she arrived to open for the day's trading, and after introducing himself as Detective Stoker, he followed her into the building.

"What can I do for you?" Lucija asked, warily, as she sat down behind her counter. The detective did not immediately respond. Instead he picked up an embroidered bookmark from a small box on the counter and flicked it nimbly between his fingers.

"One and six for this?" he said, after a while.

"A local charwoman makes them. The money goes to, oh, needy orphans or some such, I imagine. Look, what's this about?"

Stoker sniffed, dropped the bookmark back into its box and then leant forward onto the counter. He was a man of hefty build and the wood creaked in protest. "I've heard things about you, Miss Gibbons," he said. "Little rumours, bits of talk here and there."

"The opium den? The bodies buried in the backyard?"

He regarded her without amusement. "The fact of the matter is you've been importing certain books, that's the fact of the matter."

Lucija gestured about her. "It's a bookshop."

"Filthy books. Illegal books. Indecent books, to get to the legal point. Objectionable matter that the ordinary self-respecting citizen should not be exposed to. You can dress it up how you like, it might as well be opium given the harm it will do." He leaned forward further, making the counter groan. "General Order nine-seven-eight," he concluded, heavily.

Lucija snorted derisively. "The law that says we're only allowed to read books suitable for our children?"

Stoker remained undaunted. "Not that you have any, Miss. Might do you good if you had. Now, would you like me to have a look under your counter there, or out the back? I wonder what I might turn up?"

"Dust, mostly, I would imagine. Look, is this really the best use of your time, Detective?" she demanded. "Haven't you anything else you could be doing?"

"Ah, well, now we're getting down to it." He scratched idly at one monstrous sideburn. "Your brothers and your father, Miss Gibbons. Rather political family, aren't you?"

Lucija crossed her arms, waiting. After a brief pause, Stoker continued.

"They're involved in a few things, are your brothers. Got their fingers in quite a few pies." Rather absurdly he slowly mimed a man sticking his finger into a pie.

"So?"

"So they're Communists, Miss Gibbons, as you well know. Now, I'm here to suggest a little arrangement. You have a little chat with your brothers, maybe your old dad too, and you come and tell me what they're up to. Otherwise I might have to come back and have a good look at your stock and maybe set Customs onto anything with your name on it that gets imported, eh?"

The shop's door swung open and Marchant came in, clutching a cardboard box full of new books.

"Oh, hello," he said, startled to see the policeman.

"Geoff, this is Detective Stoker," Lucija said, getting up again.

"I know all about *Mister* Marchant," sneered Stoker, crossing his arms. "Quite famous down the station for his nocturnal escapades." He made the finger-in-pie gesture again, even more slowly.

"What marvellous muttonchops you've grown there, Detective," Geoff replied, setting down his box. "In the theatre we used to call them 'Bugger's Grips.'"

The policeman flushed red and moved to the door.

"Think about what I said, Miss Gibbons," he said. "I'll see you soon, right?"

"Give my best to Inspector Jacob," Geoff smiled. The detective smirked.

"Jacob's been sacked," he said. "Indecent conduct. We're chatting to a few of his friends right now."

Geoff's face fell. Stoker grinned nastily and left.

§

The policeman came at me from the shadows, wielding his truncheon like a mace. I stepped to one side, only just in the nick of time, as the weapon swung over my head.

"Don't move!" yelled Detective Stokes. Unarmed, I faced off against him. He knew what I knew—that the evidence of his gross corruption was in the notebook beside poor dead Sheila's bed.

"I'll see you hang before I'm through, Rogers!" the officer snarled, running a hand over his trembling whiskers. The thick wax he used to tame them gleamed in the moonlight.

"Did you see her die?" I snarled, my hands up.

He snorted. "I'll see you die," he retorted.

I suddenly moved my right hand, as though reaching for a pistol. Stokes swung his truncheon at my wrist, but before it could connect I had already shifted sideways. I was now to his left, kicking out as hard as I could. His weapon clattered to the paving stones, followed closely by his knees and face. I snatched up the truncheon and stood over him, blocking the moonlight from his frightened face.

"Detective Stokes," I said, smiling. "I'm going to give you the well-deserved thrashing of a lifetime."

§

"I'm Captain Moonlight!" shrilled the little boy, bounding down the steps toward her with his cap gun in his hands. "Hand over all your gold!"

Lucija laughed and picked Edgar up. His stocky little body squirmed in her strong arms as he tried to evade his aunt's sloppy kiss.

"Captain Moonlight never hurt the ladies," she told him. "Is your pa about?"

The diminutive bushranger took her through to the back of the house, where Matej was throwing feed to the chickens. "To what do I owe this honour?" he asked, hens about his feet.

"If I were to go away for a while, would you take the cats and the peacock?" Lucija asked. "Jean's not keen on the animals, I shouldn't like to think of them left uncared for. Petar doesn't have the space, but you do."

"Go away? What's all this?"

"I'm selling the shop—I've an appointment with one of Geoff's lawyer friends this afternoon, sorting out all the intricacies. I was thinking of travelling to London."

"London?" he boggled. "But you love that shop! What's going on here, Lucy?"

She shrugged and hedged around the truth. "I've a feeling business is going to go downhill, so I'm getting out while I'm ahead. You might want to be a bit more careful, too."

"Is this that bastard Stoker?"

"He's being very persistent, and I don't think he's going to give up. Trade's on a knife edge as it is, so if he makes trouble I could lose everything. I'd rather sell up and have a little money."

"That fucking bloody fucking bloody shit!"

"Well, quite."

Matej scowled and kicked the feed bin. "I'd better get Dad to lay low for a bit, eh?"

"It might be wise."

"And London?"

"That's Geoff's idea. He was going there anyway to

try and organise some overseas sales of his books. This all just makes it a bit more pressing."

Matej led his sister to the chairs on the back veranda.

"Listen, Lucy, you're not sweet on Geoff Marchant, are you?"

She laughed. "What?"

"Well, he's a top fella, I wouldn't say a word against him, but he's... well, Lucy, he's the biggest poofter in the land!"

"You idiot! And what do you think I am?"

He gaped. "But you're a woman!"

"God, you're more like Queen Victoria than you know, Matty."

He paled. "You and Jean, you're not..."

She laughed again. "Of course not. You really are a fathead. There's nobody, not really. Nobody important. So I'm free to leave as soon as I can sort the shop out."

"Bloody hell. I need a drink."

"I'll have one too, thanks. While you're up."

§

After what would be the last day of posing and painting, and once Jean was dressed again, she came over for a final look at the latest painting in progress.

"That's meant to be my arm, is it?"

Simpkins flushed and glowered. "Of course it is," he muttered.

"How many joints do you think I have?"

"Oh, shut up!"

Nodding to herself, Jean straightened her clothes. Then she pointed at the murky nude's belly.

"I'm pregnant, you know," she said. Simpkins gaped

and quivered, then recovered rapidly.

"Ah, well, you see...," he began, then stopped.

"Yes? What do I see?"

"It's just... Well, I've a passage booked for Auckland next week, you know."

"What is it that you think I'm telling you?"

Simpkins stepped onto the mine, knowing he was doing so but unable to see how not to. "That you want to get married?"

He fell, stunned by pain and surprise. Jean's well-aimed blow had caught him in the solar plexus. "Nngh," he managed, quietly, from his small world of pain.

"I have no interest in you being his *father*," Jean said scornfully. "I want a child, not another bloody husband!"

"Nngh?"

"I just wondered whether you'd have the decency to *try* to summon a little nobility, or at least a little cash to help with expenses. Obviously not, though I suppose I'm a fool for thinking you might react in any other way. You still owe me six pounds for modelling, by the way."

Once the money was folded away in her purse, Jean paused at the top of the stairs to look back over the studio.

"You haven't an ounce of talent at all, you know," she said. "Even a naïve colonial girl can see that."

§

The child was born in the bedroom Jean had taken in Matej's house. Her sister-in-law was an old hand at childbirth, and an effective midwife. Jean called the baby Beatrice.

Dick Rogers' new publisher, a dull but financially

brilliant fellow who had been an old school friend of Marchant's, delivered flowers and a polite note of congratulation. His predecessor wired an obscurely obscene poem from London.

Jean taught Beatrice to read from an early age. Lucija's weekly letters each finished with a brief list of "suggested reading," beautiful picture books which would arrive in big monthly packages from the London bookshop in which she was now working.

At night Jean took the infant out among the blue-gums and named the plants and the animals, including those (cats, peacock) which had moved with her from the big house in Randwick, an alphabet book of life.

One Bloody Thing After Another

CHRISTINE TAPE 1

The Christmas before it happened was the last time we were all together. God. What a year. I was looking in my diary before you came. Singapore fell to the Japs, Darwin was bombed by them too, and they had those submarines shelling Sydney Harbour. The Kokoda Trail. And then that bloody Christmas, which I was hosting, of course. It was always muggins here hosting.

Well, I say all together, but Kenneth was in New Guinea, and Bernard was too, in the Army. But the others were there, and Dad and Uncle Neil, and that's who you're most interested in, isn't it?

Well, yes, exactly.

So there were four of us Gibbons kids, though that Christmas we were all grown-ups of course. Annie, she was the oldest, though you wouldn't know it by the way she carried on. Such a pain. Bernard, who was away as I said. Me. And poor David.

Don't know why they did that. Annie, Bernard, Christine, David, alphabetical order the order we were born in. It wasn't like Dad to be playful like that, so it must have been Mum, but she was dead so I never got to ask her.

God, no, not Dad. I'm amazed he didn't just call us Boy One, Boy Two, Girl One and so forth. You know what I mean. Though even that would have been funny, and he wasn't ever what you'd call a funny man.

Is it recording? Oh yes, the little wheels are turning.

Dad and Uncle Neil showed up in a shiny new car. Fresh from their yard, no doubt. They had one of the biggest car yards in Adelaide, which is of course what led to all the trouble. They must have both been in their forties, but you wouldn't know it in either case. Dad must have been born looking sixty, and Uncle Neil still sort of looked like a kid. Loud trousers, long hair, sort of fashionable-unfashionable, if you know what I mean.

No, the poor man, more than anything he wanted to be nicknamed "Hollywood." I remember he was always trying to get people to call him that. Hollywood Gibbons, for God's sake. Always doing tricks with his cigarettes and toothpicks, flicking them round between his fingers like a magician. He was quite good, actually. Whereas Dad just did his crossword puzzles.

The house was near Port Augusta, by the beach. A bit of a drive for everyone from Adelaide, but most of them came up by train. Bernard's wife brought their kids. You need the little ones around at Christmas. We did, anyway, otherwise it would have been unbearable. Can you imagine?

No, I suppose you can't.

No, Jean and Beatrice weren't there. I don't think I ever saw Dad and Aunt Jean in a room together. Jean had no husband, Beatrice was a bastard, so that was that.

Her books? Where did you find them? I don't think I have any copies of any of them any more.

Oh, yes, I suppose you can get all sorts of things on the computer these days.

Don't make fun of me! I can't help being old-fashioned. I'm old!

I suppose most of us thought the Japanese would probably invade in the new year. I know I did. I mean,

Adelaide's a long way from the east coast but there's no way we'd have been left alone if it happened. Absolute nightmare when you saw what they were doing everywhere else they'd taken over. Horrible. So that cast a pall, as you can imagine.

I was in the Land Army. With Kenneth away in New Guinea and no kids to look after, I had to do something useful. A poultry farm. Eggs, mostly. It wasn't what I'd call fun, but it passed the time.

Well, I was very lonely. There was this shed on the farm nobody used for anything. Sometimes I'd just go in there and scream.

No, I'd never heard of James Harold then. None of us had. I mean, Dad and Neil had a lot of customers.

§

and he spends Christmas Day drinking with the curtains closed and he knows he can't afford to waste what little money he has on the booze but for once he's going to spend something on himself and damn the consequences and what does he pay maintenance for anyway eight kids and he hasn't seen seven of them in more than a year and today all of them would be on the farm with his wife and all he has is the booze and the letter from the Welfare people and the letter from the Gibbons brothers so much money and so he has another drink and another drink after that

§

ANNIE TAPE 1

Ha, war work was not for me, I can tell you that!

Christine was grubbing around with the chooks most of the war, but I had a proper job. Yes, running the office for Dad and Neil.

"Hollywood"? God, yes, he desperately wanted to be called Hollywood. Poor man, all he really wanted was to be liked. And go to the movies. He was always saying, "Ducks,"—that's what he always called me—"Ducks, can you check what's playing for me?"

No, I'm not really sure what Neil did other than sort of hang around. But he'd put in half the money so it wasn't as though Dad could fire him. He'd have loved to, I'm sure. Neil was too soft-hearted, always giving people the benefit of the doubt.

Taking advantage, that's what happened. You show you're soft, you show you're weak, and people walk all over you. That's why Dad wouldn't let James Harold talk to him, always dealt with him himself. The man always had some excuse—his wife, his kids, his back, no job, whatever.

§

and it was the first miscarriage that started it she'd had eight babies safely and then miscarriage after miscarriage something gone wrong and she started blaming him as though somehow he caused them calling him a baby killer she'd actually gone mad he remembered thinking that for the first time not believing it and then each day some new evidence and she couldn't even look at him without disgust and the farm getting more and more into debt nothing working out right so he took off for Adelaide to find paying work sold the horse as soon as he got into town and made the mistake of buying a car so he could get to jobs easier and who does he buy from the fucking Gibbons brothers worst mistake of his life

§

WILLIAM TAPE 1

I have nothing to say. No, I don't wish to discuss this at all.

§

and he had the letters from the Gibbons piling up enough for a book he sometimes thought he owed them so much and the interest kept on climbing and he even went to beg with them more than once swallowing his pride and he did it and William Gibbons pushed him actually pushed him out the door yelling in his face you've got to pay up man do you want to go to gaol so much *and he fell back tripping on the step and he fell back and hurt his back the pain was incredible he actually burst into tears as though he had any more dignity left to lose and yet there he was lying in the dust with William and Neil Gibbons staring down at him the younger one with his cigarette and fancy suit and his* steady on Bill there's no need for that *the older one like a judge in the Bible and he was just scrabbling around like a kid and his pants were torn they were so keen to kick a man when he was down that they'd ruin his only pair of pants and how would he find a job now and life was just one bloody thing after another there was always further to fall*

§

I was in New Guinea, in the army, at that time, so I'd never heard of the man. Other things on my mind.

Yes, exactly that.

I got letters from Christine quite often. They were pretty welcome, it gave you a sense of normal-ish things happening *somewhere*, but there was always something a bit, I don't know, brittle about them? Like someone determined to make polite conversation in a burning building.

You know what I mean.

Yeah, Neil wrote occasionally. He'd send a bit of gossip. Some chat about some actress's legs or whatever.

Dad? No. I don't think he was the kind to write letters. Or not ones that weren't demanding someone pay up.

§

and he caught the 8:14 morning train from the Blackwood station sitting in breathless silence schoolchildren rioting around him in the confined space shocking language some of them were his own kids talking like this and he tries to think about what he's doing but it's like trying to recall a dream his mind just skitters away from this void at the centre of his thoughts he's almost moving like an automaton now he hasn't taken the fatal step yet but it feels already done he's just a marble rolling down its track and the weight of the revolver in his pocket should feel familiar he was a soldier after all though he never made it further than Durban before peace was declared but it feels odd now as though that whole side of his body is experiencing too much gravity and he gets out in the city walking past the underground tobacconists and newsagents and into the warm sun another lovely day

§

ANNIE TAPE 1

They'd asked me to get the lunch, I did that every day pretty much except Fridays and Saturdays when they went out. But I was still in the office getting petty cash out of the box. We used to keep it in a drawer but someone snatched it once, this kid who still owed ten pounds for his motorbike. As though he wouldn't be easy to track down. People don't think.

Yes, so James Harold came in. He looked very strange. Sort of sweaty and pale, like he had food poisoning. Dad just marched right over and started yelling. "Have you brought my money?" or "Where's my money?"... Something along those lines. He began to push Harold out of the door.

Dad was a big man.

Well, then suddenly Dad was coming back in backwards, like the film was going into reverse, and Harold's pointing this gun at him. I dropped the box, there was this crash, I think I thought it was the gun going off but it wasn't. But then he did pull the trigger, and it just went click. So he pulled it again and it just clicked again.

Well they say that about revolvers but obviously it can happen.

No. It can only have been maybe a second or two but your brain behaves weirdly. I remember having time to think whole sentences, we were going to die, no we weren't, the gun was broken, we were saved, should I call the police? All of that.

So Uncle Neil stood up. And Dad just ran out the back door with a sort of shout. Like, waaurgh, sort of like that. Yes. And James Harold was like a man with a blocked hose. He was looking down the barrel with this confused look on his face. Then he shook it, the gun, shook it again, and it went off. And Uncle Neil just went over backwards, over the back of his chair.

Yes. "Ducks?" he said. "Ducks, call the police, I've been shot."

§

and he walks sedately up to the charge window of the city watchhouse knocks politely until someone comes to see what he wants and he takes out the revolver and puts it on the desk and explains himself I've just cleaned up one of the Gibbons brothers in Gawler Place if it's of any interest to you and I would have got the other one if this damn thing hadn't jammed *and the detective they take him to takes a long time to ask him anything he seems so surprised and then he asks* why did you come here *and he has to explain* to save you blokes the trouble of looking for me I'm all done now *and when he's asked why he's suddenly so tired it should be over now and having to explain himself is almost more than he can bear and he just wants to sleep but he has to talk* I consider them rats without a drop of human kindness in them I never did anyone any harm anyone I know will tell you that and they've ruined me ruined my life *and the detective has been handed a report and he says* I think the man you shot will die you will be charged with murder have you thought of that *and he says* yes I have thought of that for a long time sir *and they take him down to the cells*

§

CHRISTINE TAPE 2

So many letters, you wouldn't believe it. As though I had any power.

I think it was my cousins who started it. Petar and Matej, did you ever meet them? Communists, quite high up in the party. Well, Matej was. I think Petar might have been in prison at the time, he was in and out a bit for political stuff.

Me? God, no.

Well, they had all these people writing to me from the Communist Party, all this "can you see it in your heart to spare the life of James Harold?" crap. How I could set a good example as a family member if I asked for clemency. They had people out in the Anzac Day march that year, handing out leaflets about it. A couple of unions got involved, it was quite a fuss. They were writing to Annie and David too.

What could I do? Who did they think I was, a judge or a minister or something?

No, I'm sorry, you can't, I burned them all.

§

and today he can't hear anything from outside the gaol not like yesterday when they were protesting just outside the walls against his hanging all the anti-capital punishment people but today the police are outside keeping everyone away and only two people get through a woman on a bicycle trying to get a

Bible to him but she's stopped at the barricades and all she can do is pray loudly there and then there's another woman who tells the guards God has told her to take Harold's place and they need to let her in but they don't so she runs to a telephone box and tries to call the Keeper of the gaol but he won't answer and so when Harold spends his last hour in his cell with the chaplain who's about the only person he's seen anything of for the last four weeks in solitary and the chaplain takes from him the nine letters he has written one for the wife one for each of the children and the chaplain agrees to pass on Harold's thanks to the prison guards for the courtesy with which they have attended him and then Harold is on his feet and he does not know that three different munitions factories are already downing tools to protest his hanging and he's walking the corridor with his hands chained and he's already at the scaffold and he's climbing the steps and he's blindfolded and though he thought he had made his peace it's too soon and he's not ready and he panics and then it's the thunk of the trapdoor opening and he drops into infinity

Field of Thunder

He turned his back, covered his eyes, and saw his skeleton.

§

Private Gibbons dropped his millionth potato into the water and wiped his nose on the back of his hand. The interior of the huge tent was filled with steam and the smell of gas and boiled meat. "Any news?" he asked a young man with sand in his hair who had appeared through the tent flaps. "How many days 'til it goes off?"

The young man shrugged. He was stripped down to his shorts and boots, trails of dusty sweat marking his sunburnt back and chest. Under one arm he was holding a battered clipboard.

"Sorry, Dave, haven't a bloody clue. Listen, what do you fellas need in the next shipment?"

"The usual, mate, all the usual." He turned back and stirred the bobbing spuds. Private David Gibbons had never been a fighting soldier, and had no interest in becoming one. He'd cooked in Korea and he cooked out here in the South Australian desert. It was, for the most part, a soft job with decent pay, better than the warehouse work he'd done before enlisting.

"Hope they don't set it off while I'm away," he muttered to the potatoes as the supplies clerk poked around in the cupboards behind him. A couple of the other cooks clattered away near the entrance, duelling with frying pans while their superiors weren't looking.

"You got leave, eh?"

"Yeah, a few days with the wife and kid. Looking forward to it."

"Salt?"

"How much we got left?"

The young man counted sacks.

"Enough," he replied, scratching his bum with the end of his pencil. "Look, I'll let you know soon as I hear anything, right?"

Gibbons nodded his thanks and started chopping carrots. "Oughta be a hell of a show," he said.

§

There were more than three hundred mouths to feed. Operation Buffalo had been out here for months, a tent city on the edge of the Nullarbor, which was seven hundred miles of flat, scrubby desert. Gibbons had been at the camp for only a few weeks, summoned from Adelaide to replace a bloke who broke his arm.

The train journey had been long and dull. After Port Augusta the view consisted of sand and saltbush. He read the paper and joked around with the other soldiers. There was a bit of talk about Malaya. Somebody knew somebody whose brother was up in one of the Royal Air Force's Vampires, doing bombing runs to clear the way for the Australian artillery and their twenty-five-pounders, support operations to give the British time to fuck everything up in their usual fashion.

The train rattled through a series of tiny, featureless sidings twenty or thirty miles apart in the middle of nowhere: Barton, Immarna, Ooldea. At Watson they finally disembarked into a sandpaper wind. Gibbons swore and stamped his feet in the red dust, looking around at the bleak horizon. The railway line extended infinitely to the east and west, bruised iron swollen by the heat and straining against the sleepers.

He and the other soldiers stood around by the rail-line, spitting into the sand and muttering quietly about the featureless view. The train departed, headed off on its slow trek west. It was two hours before the Rovers arrived, three rusty hulks bouncing over the dunes toward them as the sun began to bleed into the flat horizon. They all packed in, sandy sardines, and the drivers set off.

As the Rovers bounced through the undulating terrain, Gibbons leaned forward from his back seat and asked the driver why all the sand ridges seemed to be lined up in the same direction.

"The fucken wind round here hasn't changed for centuries!" the man shouted back over the sound of engine and complaining suspension. "Just comes whipping across the fucken Nullarbor all the fucken time and piles all the fucken sand up."

Gibbons looked around at the desolation. The occasional dark clump of mulga drew the eye like a magnet.

"I heard some blackfellas live round here," commented one of the other soldiers, obviously bemused by the notion. "What the hell do they eat and drink?"

"Nothin' now!" bawled the driver. "Had to fucken round 'em up and get 'em to fucken shoot off. Poor fucken buggers just didn't understand what was going on. Thought they were gunna be fucken bombed by some foreign fucken country. Couldn't figure out why Australia would be fucken bombing itself."

Gibbons laughed. "Well, we're technically being bombed by the bloody British, aren't we? Fucken Poms."

"True enough, mate."

The Rovers lurched on, long shadows rippling away to the right, headed for Maralinga.

§

On his first night home on leave they were both too tired to want to have sex but did it anyway, thinking they ought to. It was not a huge success. Afterwards they lay naked and awake, breathing in the smell of the paint Tabitha had recently applied to the bedroom walls.

"So what are you all up to out there, anyway?" she asked, lighting his cigarette from her own.

"The bloody Poms are setting off atom bombs."

"You're a poet and you don't know it," Tabitha replied, automatically. "Is it dangerous?" David shrugged and tipped his head back, puffing a stream of smoke towards the ceiling. "Only if you get too close. I'm hoping they don't do the next one before I get back. It sounds like an impressive bang."

"David…"

His name hung there between them, forcing him to narrow his attention. "What?"

"I know we've talked about this before, but … Suzie's getting big and she needs new clothes all the time and I'm thinking I might have to get work too."

"No. We've been through all this, love."

"But I just spend all my time bumbling around the house! Suzie's at school all day. Look, you remember Jane at the library? She says they're looking for somebody else, and I was thinking I could…"

David shook his head. "No! Look, why? There's enough money—I know it gets a bit tight, but we manage. It's my job to be the provider, and I'm providing."

"It would only be a couple of days each week..."

David turned onto his side, facing away from her. "I'm tired, Tab. Can we talk about this in the morning?"

She sighed and got out of bed, pulling on her knickers and going out to the toilet. David stubbed out his cigarette and shut his eyes against the darkness.

§

"New shoes, Dad! I hate these!"

David made a sour face. "You can't just get new things every time you feel like it, Sunshine."

Tabitha took her daughter's hand and squeezed it. "Actually, she *does* need new ones. The ones she's got are falling apart on her feet."

The three of them walked up the south side of Rundle Street, window-shopping. David annoyed his wife by ducking into the army surplus shop, while he sighed theatrically as she admired a new coat. It wasn't as though it was even winter. Suzie hung between them, pouting and uttering impatient commentary. She'd been given the day off school to celebrate her dad's return, and didn't want to waste it dawdling around boring grown-up shops.

David treated his family to ice cream from the shop on the corner. They loitered in the shade of the canvas awning while David pointed at the things that had changed since he'd last been here.

In a bookshop he bought a couple of potboilers while

Suzie rampaged through the children's books. Picking through the racks of murder mysteries, David wondered whether his mad Aunt Jean was still writing. She always used pseudonyms, as far as he knew, and he couldn't remember what any of them were.

The shoe shop next door held an unexpected marvel. In the centre of the floor, surrounded by racks of slippers and sandals, boots and high-heels, stood a wooden, blockish object roughly half David's height. Smiling, he took the others over to it.

"Put your feet in there," he said, indicating the hole at the base of the block. Suzie did so, frowning and wondering what the trick was. "Now look in there," he added, indicating the eyepiece mounted on the top of the box, looking inward. Suzie pressed her face to the padding, still puzzled, and David reached down to flick the switch.

His daughter gave a gasp of amazement as she saw the bones of her feet, bright against the blue-black darkness. She wriggled her toes in the X-ray glow, watching the movement of her tiny bones. She could even see the nails and stitches in the outline of her shoes. David gave a pleased laugh at her reaction, and Tabitha gave him the first friendly smile she had shown all day.

"Let's get you some new shoes, Sunshine, and then you can look at them in the machine again, eh?"

§

On Tuesday morning he reported to the barracks with his bags packed and his uniform freshly laundered. Rather than bothering walking all the way round to the gate, he jumped the chain fence and walked across lawns. A defunct old artillery piece loomed on his right, aimed out across the road towards the river.

The barracks were next to the university, and below a lush green slope which led up to the stone walls around the Governor's residence. He could hear the music of a pipe band; some official function or other.

A squad of trainees was drilling in the morning sun, rifles swinging as the soldiers turned and marched. He didn't envy them. For all the heat and dust and boredom, Gibbons enjoyed the relative laxness of Maralinga. He went in through the main entrance and reported to the main desk. Tabitha would be walking home now, having dropped Suzie at the school gates. David missed them, but didn't regret his return to duty. It felt like pulling on comfortable old clothes.

"Davie!" called a voice from behind him. He turned.

"Morris! Where've you been the last few months?"

"Up north, mate, bloody Queensland. You heading back to Operation Buffalo?"

"Yeah, just come off leave."

"Bewdy, Davie! I'm off there meself. Be just like old times. You still cooking?"

"Of course."

Morris turned to the scowling sergeant behind the desk.

"This bloke does things with offal you wouldn't believe, Sarge," he smirked, slinging an arm round Gibbons' neck. The sergeant's scowl deepened and he licked the end of his pen, leaving a stain of ink on the end of his tongue.

"Names?" he demanded. David nudged his mate, feeling like a schoolboy in trouble with the teacher.

"Private Brian Morris, sir!"

"Private David Gibbons, sir!"

The sergeant gestured down the hallway.

"Get yourselves sorted, boys. Train's off in an hour."

§

Five days later, and another shift in the cooking tent. Pea and ham soup gave everything a morning urine odour.

"Bloody pathetic," remarked Morris, who was hiding from his senior officer after a dispute. His uniform was dust-coated and mud-streaked. His tobacco-stained fingertips tapped against the pile of uncooked vegetables. "You've never seen such a sad bloody sight."

Private Gibbons nodded without speaking.

"There was a whole family of the poor beggars camped out on the edge of one of the bomb craters," Morris continued. "Didn't have a clue what was going on. We told 'em they'd better bugger off before today's test or they'd be sorry. They said they thought the crater was the 'Great Snake' digging holes."

Gibbons hadn't had any contact with the locals. Despite their officially having been moved on from Maralinga, it was a huge area, and there were only two patrol officers making sure that nobody was getting back in.

"The test's definitely on for this afternoon?" he asked.

"You bet, sport."

"What if some of them stray back into the range?"

Morris shrugged. "Blowed if I know, mate. Just glad it's not me's gotta keep an eye on 'em."

Somebody barged in through the partly closed flaps, rubbing his hands together. "Oi! Flag's up, boys! Muster in the parade ground, chop-chop! Here we fucken go!"

Morris grinned. "At bloody last. This'll be something to tell the grandkids, eh?"

They went outside, joining the noisy stream of men pushing between the tents towards the beaten flat earth of the parade ground. Section heads started yelling names and checking them off on security lists. Several trucks were roaring past them, carting last-minute bits of equipment to and from the detonation site. In the remote distance, David could see a faint metallic gleam, the bomb being winched up the test tower.

The wind was coming from the south-east. The scientists had been waiting for days for the right conditions. David saw an old Centurion tank being driven out onto the fringes of the estimated blast area, its engine to be left running to see what effect the blast might have on it. "Cecil," a straw dummy made especially for the purpose, was to be left at the controls. Most of the cooks and mechanics were there in the crowd, even though they were supposed to be staying back in the tent village to help minimize the fuss. Nobody wanted to miss the show, though, and the security officers were turning a blind eye. David smiled at one of them, then pretended to hide his face behind his battered hat.

Orders were being issued through the big double loudspeakers wired up to the mulga trees, but it was hard to hear them over the excited chatter. Some of the men here had already seen one of the previous blasts, but most had not, and in any case this was scheduled to be the biggest bang yet.

More lorries pushed through the crowd, carrying the film technicians out to the camera towers. "Jesus, it's better than the Christmas Pageant, eh?" Morris laughed, reappearing at David's side. Once again he'd given his commanding officer the slip. "They oughta sell bloody tickets." He had snatched a pair of binoculars from somewhere. David borrowed them and peered through at the distant dark mass of the bomb atop its tower. It was just over four miles away, rising from the bleak desert horizon.

A Canberra bomber jet was up now, circling overhead. The pilot was to fly away from the tower in the last few seconds before the blast, and then turn back and soar through the middle of the mushroom cloud, gathering air samples and talking into a tape recorder, before screaming off to Woomera for a medical checkup. There had been quite a few volunteers for this job.

Morris muttered something excitedly and took back his binoculars. The loudspeakers announced the countdown.

"Five minutes to go."

"Okay, men, when the countdown reaches ten seconds you're to turn and face away from the blast!" an officer was shouting, walking along in front of the ranked and shuffling troops. "Only turn round again once the first flash of light has passed, right? This thing'll be brighter than the sun and you've only got one set of eyes each."

Gibbons shivered with anticipation. Morris was uncharacteristically quiet, staring out over the dust and scrubby little quandong bushes to the bomb tower.

"Two minutes to go!"

There was still a little movement out on the plain as a couple of trucks came back toward them. The jet droned overhead.

"One minute to go!"

A couple of technicians wandered past, wearing arc-welding goggles. The officer strode past again, repeating his instructions.

"I'd prefer to know what's going on than be facing away," Morris muttered, showing his nervousness for the first time. He lowered the binoculars to his chest, which was exposed under his unbuttoned jacket, and wiped his mouth with the back of his hand. "Gawd, I'd kill for a drink. Even a cuppa. Fuck, they should leave out a kettle, see if it boils in the heat."

Gibbons laughed.

"Twenty seconds to go!"

A series of rockets were set off, criss-crossing the sky over the detonation point with a grid of smoke to measure the force of the imminent shockwave. The booms took a little while to reach the waiting men, and when they did they started to turn away from the distant tower. Suddenly feeling absurdly vulnerable, Gibbons found himself pulling the collar of his shirt up around his ears and cramming his hat down harder on his head. He turned and covered his eyes with his hands, blotting out everything.

"Ten seconds to go—nine, eight, seven, six, five, four, three, two, one, now!"

There was a flash of light brighter than anything Gibbons had ever experienced. Though his eyes were closed and covered, he saw the bones of his fingers through his suddenly X-ray clear flesh. A searing burst of heat struck him on the back of the head, burning his skin. Stunned, he let his hands drop and found he could not see the camp, just an endless obliteration of impossible white light. A hole had opened in the universe, and the light from somewhere else was coming through.

Then it faded a little, and the vaguest details began to reappear. Gibbons turned back to look out across the plain. A huge fireball was boiling in on itself as it tore up into the sky, wrenching tonnes of dust and ash up with it into a huge mushroom cloud. The tiny shape of the bomber banked round and ploughed into the smoke, disappearing from view. There was no sound from the bomb yet, just the groans and shouts of the men around him.

Wide-eyed and open-mouthed, Private Gibbons saw something happening to the scattered trees on the plain, as though they were being flattened. The deformation seemed to speed up as it drew closer, and then it was upon them: a shockwave of violent, hot wind and the loudest noise any of them had ever heard. Private Gibbons was knocked down by the blast, deafened and screaming with fear.

Afterwards he went with Morris and a few others into the blast zone, staring at the scorched earth and streaks of billowing flame, the shredded remnants that used to be vegetation. Gibbons slid down the curved banks of the smoking crater, his boots breaking up a crust of glass. As he stumbled through the glazed wreckage, the seeds of a thousand future cancers took root inside his cells.

Comfort & Joy

The pram's plastic wheels juddered and skipped over the broken footpath as Katherine Gibbons headed up the street toward the bank. It was warm—the Darwin warmth that never goes away between December and March, and rarely after that—and on a Monday morning the streets were not too busy.

"Muh!" protested Frankie from the pram. "Muheeeeee!"

Katherine reached down and stroked his downy head, shushing absent-mindedly through pursed lips. She was nineteen, dark-haired and skinny in a brown cotton dress and cheap sandals. Her sunglasses, borrowed without asking from her older sister, hid tired eyes.

The bank was air-conditioned, a rare luxury in this broiler of a town. Katherine parked the pram and sat at one of the small tables against the wall, consulting her passbook and rendering two withdrawal slips illegible before finally entering the right numbers in the right boxes. She jumped up and wheeled Frankie over to the queue.

"Isn't he adorable!" swooned the old woman in front of her.

"Muh!" assented Frankie. Katherine smiled thinly.

At the counter she slouched heavily against the wood, feeling the brief reprieve of the cold varnish through her clothes.

"This closes the account," stated the teller, slow frown suggesting such a thing was unheard of.

"Yup."

"Are you sure? You only need a coupla dollars in there to keep it open."

Katherine hunched down on the counter and shook her head. Her son was playing with his feet.

"I want all of it."

The teller shrugged, a man used to talking reasonably into the uncaring void. "Sign there," he indicated, blunt thumb pressed down on the relevant box. Katherine wielded the proffered pen and pushed her passbook at the man. He sighed, stamped and counted out the money: two hundred and twelve dollars in twenties, tens and a two.

"Last-minute Christmas shopping?" he asked.

"Nup," responded Katherine. She made a show of counting the cash, flicking back the corners of the notes, then she stuffed the money in her handbag and pushed Frankie back out into the sun.

"You want an ice cream?" she asked as they hesitated outside a deli further up the street.

"Yes!"

"Mummy's gunna have some cake."

"Cack!"

They went into the shadowy building, plastic straps trailing over her bare and sweaty shoulders. Katherine picked through the freezer until she found an ice block for Frankie, then went up to the counter, where she made a show of going through her purse and coming up twenty cents short. The older woman behind the counter smiled and slapped her palms against her striped apron.

"She's right, love. 'Ave a good Christmas."

"Thanks. You too."

Then back out into the heat, with Frankie dribbling

red stickiness down his chin.

§

The stuttering chatter of the typewriter stopped when the record player's needle settled back into its cradle with a warm clunk. Edgar looked up from his desk, stabbed a comma onto the page, and then rose to flip through his record collection. It was time for something Baroque. He was about to kill off his major protagonist and he wanted an appropriate soundtrack.

Edgar Gibbons was forty-nine, an uneasy grandfather with thick white hair and six successful—and one early unsuccessful—novels to his credit. As he aged, his central characters got younger. His first book, published when he was twenty-one, had been about old men whose age and decrepitude seemed to him the most poignant thing in the world. Now Edgar looked sideways at a mid-life crisis and wrote about twenty-somethings and their sex lives.

The shelf above his desk was lined with his own books, carefully arranged in order of publication in all their different editions: the mint hardbacks and orange-spined Penguin paperbacks, the American editions with their invariably awful covers, the translations into French and Italian. His editor was talking about a set of re-releases when he finished the new one. Matching and attractive cover designs, reinvigorating the backlist.

The Albinoni concerto swelled to fill the room, sun-caught dust motes danced near the cobweb-coated speakers. He had read that Sydney was about to get stereo FM radio. How many years before backwater Darwin received this bounty of modern technology?

Edgar and Mary had moved to the tropics in the middle of the Sixties. He had been amazed to find that he could support a family on the proceeds of his books. Darwin seemed a peaceful, cheap and luxuriously slow-paced place to live and write. Katherine, their youngest, hadn't cared where they lived, as long as it had a TV. Steven and Belinda had been teenagers, and much less sanguine about it. Both had left for the east coast soon after their respective eighteenth birthdays. It took Christmas to bring them back to the Territory.

Edgar wound the page out of the typewriter and added it to the small stack on his desk, face-down, the corners square with the angles of the room. A little over one thousand words, not bad for a day when inspiration had seemed sluggish. He had little enough to do before finishing this rewrite, but as the final page drew closer he always found it harder to go on. He knew his writing had a certain easy glibness, that it lacked the qualities it needed to make him the sort of writer he admired. The last stages of a book, when the possibilities of greatness definitively closed down and he had to commit to a final draft, were the worst.

There was a knock at the door, and then Mary slipped in, standing in the sharp-edged stream of light with a mug in hand. Nearly fifty years had done little to fill out her angular frame. She was as slender and delicate as ever. When Katherine had become pregnant with little Frankie, Edgar had been reminded of how odd his own wife had looked with a bulbous stomach and swollen ankles on a stick-insect build.

"Cyclone warning," she said in her soft voice, bringing the coffee over and setting it down on his desk. Edgar grinned thanks, leaned back and drank.

"Always a cyclone warning, never a cyclone," he commented. "What happened to the one a week ago?"

Mary shrugged and nodded, hands on her hips as she enjoyed the warmth of the morning sun. "Won't come to anything. Probably die out to sea."

They stood in companionable silence for a minute or so, music and slurped coffee the only sounds of life. Then there was a thump from above, and the sound of a toilet flushing.

"Belinda's only just getting up?" frowned Edgar. "That girl gets lazier every year!"

"She had a long trip, love! It's a hell of a drive. Listen, she was saying last night we could go out for lunch before we pick up Steve from the airport."

Edgar nodded. "Katherine coming?"

"Who knows? I haven't seen her this morning. Honestly, she gets it from you. Always playing dumb, creeping around doing her own thing."

Edgar tried to feign hurt feelings, but his heart wasn't in it. "Do you reckon she's told Belinda or Steve who the father is?"

"I doubt it. I believe her when the silly girl says she doesn't know herself. She was all over the place before she got pregnant."

Edgar harrumphed. It was so *untidy* to not know the father of your own child, so very much the sort of thing Katherine would have to go and do.

"Yeah, well, bloody kids," he said, as good a summing up as any. "Anyway, this draft is coming on alright. I think I'll give it away for today."

Mary smiled and kissed his forehead below the shock of white hair, then turned and went out. Edgar stood and stretched before following her.

§

The plane hit the runway, wheels squealing, and then taxied towards the shambolic airport buildings. Tall palms waved in the gentle tropical breeze, beckoning to the travellers through the plane's small windows.

"Farewell Aunty Jack, we know you'll be back," Steve half-sang, half-hummed as he peered out at the baking tarmac. Sarah's grip on his arm tightened.

"Stop it!" she hissed. "You've been singing that stupid song the whole flight! You're driving me round the bloody bend!"

"Sorry!" Steve said, genuinely surprised. It had been all over the radio for weeks. You couldn't escape it. During the wait between flights at the tiny airport in Alice Springs, where bemused American servicemen wandered around smoking cigarettes and looking hopelessly for fun, the blown-out speakers had been playing it through the hot departure lounge.

They got to their feet and waited to join the slow shuffle towards the exit. Sarah took his hand and gave him an affectionate smile, which he returned. She'd never really worn jewellery, and the novelty of her engagement ring was hard against his palm. His own hand tapped against the handle of the luggage locker above their seat, in time with the music in his head.

The noon sun outside was horrific: it had an actual weight to it. They struggled toward the shade of the airport building, past old hangars with roofs of corrugated iron. A few small planes were motionless in the distance, laid up until Christmas was over.

Belinda was the first to spot them, squawking with delight and pushing through to grab Steve in a headlock.

She then turned her attention toward her future sister-in-law, gripping Sarah by the wrists and giving her an enthusiastic kiss on the cheek.

"Mum! Dad! How are you?" Steve asked, embracing them each in turn. They looked much the same as ever, his mum with her middle-aged elegance and dad with his too-young sunglasses and sensible brown trousers. Edgar clapped Steve on the back with a bruising hand.

"How long've you been here?" Steve asked his sister as they waited for their suitcases to emerge.

"I got in yesterday morning. Drove."

"All the way? Are you crazy?"

Belinda shrugged her narrow shoulders. She had the slight build of her mother but not her father's height. Her thick and red-dyed hair was cropped to an untidy few inches, a mad crown. "I gave a lift to some friends as far as Tennant Creek—they were going back to their family too—then I came the rest of the way on my own." She gave him a nudge. "We can't all afford to fly, you know."

Steve nodded, put in his place. Looking sideways, he saw Sarah engaged in merry conversation with their mother.

"Where's Kath?"

"Ha. Somewhere in town," scoffed Belinda. "She was gone when I got up this morning. Wait 'til you see little Frankie, though. He's *gorgeous!*"

"Yeah, well, you say that about all of them."

§

Mary was surprised with the speed with which her returned children made themselves at home. Belinda had already taken back the spare room, filling it with the untidy piles of belongings she had dragged with her from Sydney. Steve and his fiancée had no room of their own, and so were to be put up in the sitting room on two sofas shoved together. They left their suitcases in the corner of the room and went straight for the kitchen, desperate for food.

"How's the ABC these days?" Edgar asked his son, pouring out generous measures of Hunter Valley Riesling.

"Oh, you know, not so bad. We were a bit worried last month after the licences were abolished, but they haven't attacked our budgets, so everyone's calmed down."

"You all excited about colour?"

Steve shrugged, wolfing down the slab of thickly buttered bread and mango jam he had prepared. "The commercial networks will show it first. Anyway, what's so great about it? Who can afford a colour set? Not us."

"Katherine's been begging for one," Mary interjected, cranking up the rickety old fan. "They can't be found though, even if you can afford them. People are snapping them up as soon as they come off the boats."

"It's not worth it," Steve said. "What's the point of colour news? You don't see people complaining about black and white in their newspapers, do you?"

"I don't think they'd mind having the option."

"Ach, I just reckon we'd be better off spending money on good scripts and good directors rather than on horribly expensive colour processing, you know?"

Belinda walked in and slung her arm round her father's neck. "How's the book coming, you horrible old man?"

"Fine, thank you."

"When do we get a read of it?" Steve asked. "Sarah's been badgering me about it for weeks."

Edgar turned toward his future daughter-in-law, feeling almost childishly pleased.

"I'm a bit of a fan," she confessed. "I did a couple of your books in uni, and I've read all the others. I really like them."

Edgar laughed and rubbed his hands together. "Forget this idiot," he said, tapping his son's shoulder. "Marry *me!*"

§

Belinda was the middle child, twenty-one years old. She loved her parents and her siblings with an amused affection that mostly sustained itself by her viewing them as though they were characters she was fond of in a likeable situation comedy. Now she jumped down from the verandah into the damp earth of the recently watered garden, landing behind her brother. Steve looked up, surprised, and smiled at her from where he was kneeling down, stroking the arched back of the neighbours' Siamese.

"What'd you get me for Christmas?"

Steve smiled and straightened. The cat transferred its attention to Belinda, insinuating its sleek self between her bare legs.

"Cup of cold fat with a hair in it. What'd you get for me?"

"Oh, the same."

They began to walk around the garden. Three years separated them. In character they were much alike, and both puzzled by the erratic obstinacy of their younger sister.

"You still enjoying life at the ABC?"

"Oh, definitely. I've got three new shows coming up next year. Couple of dramas and a comedy."

"Any cop shows?"

He smiled. "Of course. Always need more cop shows."

"So, you able to tell me what a script editor actually *does*?"

"Only if you tell me how a politician's aide makes the world a better place."

They walked on a little. As they passed the open kitchen window they could hear their mother's voice raised in unconscious song. They stopped to listen. Mary would never sing when she thought she had an audience.

"The wrinklies seem well," Steve commented.

"Yeah. Mum's looking good, isn't she?"

"And Dad never changes."

Belinda smirked. "Sarah's gone down well. You noticed how polite they're being? Dad's not even roamed the passage in his undies, at least not yet."

"Well, thank God they're trying. Sarah was really nervous before we left, you know. Meeting the future in-laws. She really wants you and Katherine to like her, too."

"Hey, she's lovely. You've done very well for yourself."

"Ta very much."

"This bloody heat, 'eh?"

"The place isn't designed for humans."

"Ha!" She pointed at his jeans. "You been into town recently? Singlets and stubbies as far as they eye can see. Only way to survive."

"I haven't sunk that low."

"Ooh, who's all hoity-toity now he's living in the big

smoke?"

"Ah, shut up."

"Too good for the clothes of the Common Man, are we?"

"Get fucked."

"Oh ho ho ho."

"Speaking of which, anyone on your horizon?" Steve asked.

"Maybe. Maybe a bit nearer, if you know what I mean."

"Oh! Visual range?"

"Arm's reach, more like it."

"Well well, you saucy wench! Tell me more."

"Oh, *al*right," Belinda sighed, with mock weariness. "He works in the office, juggles the money and sorts out the mailing lists. Almost as clever and good looking as me."

"Surely not! Could such a paragon exist?"

"Hard to believe, ain't it? Nah, he's lovely." She hesitated. "And married, of course."

Steve stopped walking and slapped himself on the forehead.

"God, Belinda, not again! Can't you find someone single?"

She shrugged. "He found me, not the other way around. Anyway, all the single guys I know are such jokes! They all want to be in bands or think they're artists. At least you know a married man has grown up a bit."

"Yeah, very responsible if he's having an affair."

"OK, Mum."

§

A wave of dark, streaking clouds preceded nightfall as the family gathered together in the sitting room. There was still no sign of Katherine. Sarah, who was reading Edgar's first draft, sat on the sofa with the pile of typed pages on her lap. Mary clattered around in the kitchen, assaulting lettuce and tomatoes, while Steve and Belinda argued their way through their childhood record collections.

"No way did I ever buy 'These Boots Are Made for Walking'!"

"Well, it's not *mine!*"

"Actually, it's mine!" their mother shouted from the kitchen.

"Haw haw, nice one, Mum!"

"What's wrong with it?"

"You're so *square*, Mother!"

"Don't make fun of your mother," Edgar chided, coming down the stairs. "What's for dinner, love?"

"Salad and more salad. I've spent days making stuff for tomorrow and Christmas Day, so it's just salad tonight. Nobody touch the chicken in the fridge!"

"Wouldn't dream of it," said Steve, extracting another clutch of 45s from the cupboard and fanning them out around him on the carpet. "Are these mine?"

Belinda inspected them. "'Hey Jude' is mine. Dunno about the rest."

"What sort of fucking name is 'Pigmeat Markham'?"

"Hmm. Better than 'Professor Morrison's Lollipop.'"

The front door opened and Katherine came in, wheeling Frankie ahead of her. Steve jumped up to greet her, while Belinda and Sarah crowded the pram and began to coo.

"Where've you been?" her father demanded. "Steve

got here hours ago!"

"Out!" snapped Katherine through her brother's embrace. She perfunctorily hugged back, then watched the girls with hawkish caution.

The six of them crowded the old dining table to eat, with Frankie in a high chair playing with his mashed potatoes behind his mother's seat.

"Pass the spuds... Cheers."

"This looks lovely, Missus Gibbons." "Thank you, Sarah."

"What's on telly?"

"We're not watching television while we eat, Katherine. How many times, eh?"

"Calm down, Edgar."

"I'm perfectly calm!"

"Amazed dad hasn't given us the Marxist reasoning on not watching TV with dinner."

"Oh, here we go."

"What?"

"You had to mention Marx."

"Did you know he had horrible piles?" Edgar asked. "Used to deal with them by putting down newspaper in the sitting room—to catch the blood—and then hacking at them with a pair of scissors."

"Fuck me, we're eating here," muttered Belinda.

Steve laughed. "I was reading this thing about Stalin, it's probably too good to be true but I hope it is. He was really into those comedy records, you know, the ones where they use dogs barking to make the tune?"

"Oh, like dogs barking 'Happy Birthday'?"

"Yeah, exactly. Anyway, he used to make underlings dance to these records for his amusement."

"Haha, he what?"

"That can't be true!"

Katherine stood up abruptly and took Frankie from his high chair, settling him down on her lap. Then, without saying anything, she undid the first few buttons of her dress and exposed one breast, pressing the child's lips to it. The conversation ground to a halt.

"Uh, isn't he a bit old for that?" Steve asked. Katherine shot him an angry look. "No," she snapped. "It's good for him."

The two men shifted uncomfortably in their seats, then Steve jumped up and went to the fridge. Edgar followed, rooting around for a fresh bottle of white. Belinda, Sarah and Mary exchanged amused looks.

After dinner, Edgar thumped the well-worn family dictionary down on the table and grinned at his offspring.

"Right then, a dollar to anybody who can tell me the meaning of...," he flipped through the pages, "... vermiculation!"

"Easy," said Belinda, smugly. "Being eaten by worms."

"Correct! Okay, how about... fubsy?"

Belinda and Steve began guessing, while Mary watched on with a smile. Sarah, surprised by this old family game, had a bemused expression. Katherine, who hated the game, gave a melodramatic sigh and stood up, still clutching Frankie.

"I'm going out!" she announced. "See you later."

"Oh, Katherine, please, stay!" protested her mother. "This is the first time we've all been together for a year! Stay and be company!"

"You've got each other for company," replied the youngest daughter, settling her son into his pram. "I'm meeting some people."

"Please, Kath, stay!" cried Belinda, getting up. "I've hardly seen you!"

Katherine shrugged this off and left, banging the front door shut behind her. The others sat in surprised attitudes, glancing at each other.

"What the fuck's wrong with her?" muttered Steve. "Language!" snapped his mother.

"I *was* using language!"

§

Katherine met the van two streets away. She had been waiting for ten minutes against the dark backdrop of a hedge, pushing Frankie's pram back and forth and singing nonsense to him.

"Ten-nine-eight-seven-six, this is very fucking dull, five-four-three-two-one, this is very fucking dull."

"Hey, hop in!" called a hoarse voice as the van she'd been waiting for finally pulled up. It was a half-wrecked old Kombi painted with a mess of psychedelia. A spattered iconography of yings, yangs, flowers, and smiley faces covered the doors. Katherine pulled open the rear door and got in, Frankie under one arm and the collapsed pram under the other.

There were two other women in the back with her, both in their twenties, perhaps sisters. They had bleached blonde hair, somewhat matted, and barely seemed to register her appearance. Quartz was driving, a truly astonishing joint clamped into his mouth.

"Kath, babe, this is Stellar and Mango," he said, forcing the recalcitrant vehicle into gear and moving off. Katherine pinched the joint from him. Headlights cut the darkness of the nearly deserted streets.

"Where we headed?" Katherine asked.

"Up on the bluff," Quartz wheezed. "We got a camp there, where Dougie's got his still? And we've got some really potent shit too."

Mango nodded and smiled sleepily. "Nobody bothers us up there," she mumbled. "Nice place."

"Yeah," commented Stellar, leaning back against the van's inner wall and idly snapping her thongs against her heels. "You'll love it."

Mango took the joint and sucked on it for a while, eyes closed. Then she handed it over to her friend and pouted a stream of smoke into Frankie's face. The tiny eyes screwed up and he sneezed a series of dainty sneezes. Katherine leaned over and slapped the girl's face.

"Don't do that!" she yelled. "He's just a kid."

"Jesus, be cool!" muttered Stellar, hardly reacting to the slap and tapping ash onto the threadbare carpet. "Just mucking round, right?"

The Kombi hit a dirt track and vibrated up the slope.

§

At a few minutes past midnight, on the morning of Christmas Eve, Sarah lay awake in the dark, wrestling with Steve on the narrow couch.

"Shsh!" she giggled, breathlessly. "Not here!"

"Why not?" he hissed back.

"It's your parents' couch, you perv! I'm not doing it here!"

"They won't know!" Steve protested. "So they won't mind!"

"*I* mind! There's not even a bloody door, anyone could walk in."

"It'll be fine!"

"Not if your parents or your sister see us it won't. I'd have to leave the country."

They settled down, elbows and knees clashing under the naphthalene-drenched blankets Mary had hauled out of an upstairs cupboard. Belinda, having arrived a day earlier, had refused to give up the spare room to them.

Sarah and Steve had met in the staff cafeteria at the ABC in Melbourne. She was a researcher for the radio news, fighting with the defensive archivists for access to old recordings. She'd been relaxing with a book and a sandwich when a young man she'd seen once or twice before came over and introduced himself as the son of the author of the book in her hands.

"So you're the kind of guy who uses his dad as a sexual lubricant?" she had replied, which had somehow failed to put him off. Now they had been engaged for three months. They looked more alike than either did to their own sisters. Both had fine brown hair and round faces.

"You don't have to be quite so complimentary to Dad," Steve suggested now, rubbing her arms.

"What? You jealous?"

"No, of course not."

"That's very Freudian."

"Oh, fuck Freud."

§

Edgar and Mary lay awake in the grey pre-dawn gloom.

"It's nice to have everyone home again," Mary said.

"Did *Katherine* come home?" Edgar demanded. The bedroom's two wide windows were fully open, and a lukewarm breeze wafted through the fly-speckled screen. A mosquito whined, infinitely.

"I didn't hear her come in," Mary replied, quietly. She could feel her husband tensing beside her. "Stop fretting. She'll be home. She always comes back."

"Why's she so bloody inconsiderate? Tell me that!"

Mary sighed. It felt as though this was fundamentally the same conversation the two of them had a dozen times a day.

"Don't get all worked up, love. You don't want to spoil Christmas."

"Me?" squawked Edgar. "I'm not the one pissing off every night!"

She sighed again and rolled onto her other side, her bony bottom pushing back against Edgar's legs. He reached out to pat her thigh, feeling slightly sheepish.

"I'm sorry," he breathed into her neck. "I just... We hardly ever see all the kids these days. I want them to remember us well, you know? I want them to have happy memories of the time we do get to spend together. Doesn't work if she's never here."

"Or if you argue with her whenever she is."

Outside the early frogs started to croak, and others swiftly joined them. The first frenzy of noise was beginning.

§

First light on Christmas Eve found Katherine with

the crown of her head jammed against a fallen palm trunk, her dress rolled up past her waist. Quartz grunted and thrust between her thighs, his dirt-smeared palms kneading her bare, grass-prickled buttocks. Her eyes were shut. Frankie slept a few metres away, rolled up in a knot of blankets.

"Unh! Unh! Unh! Unh! Babe! Unh! *Uuhnnh!*" Quartz said, before falling still, his damp lips pressed to her collar bone. Katherine opened her eyes to the breaking sunlight and pushed him off, coughing throatily to herself. Quartz sprawled out in the long grass by her side, dressed only in his well-worn blue singlet, looking extremely pleased with himself. She frowned at his sticky and unprepossessing genitals and looked away, tugging her dress down over her own. She took one of the pre-rolled cigarettes he'd made up from the pouch in his discarded shorts pocket.

The others were fifty metres down the slope behind them, still asleep in their bags. A couple of the less hardy had spent the night in the back of the Kombi. Katherine got to her bare feet and wandered off a little, trying to ignore the post-coital ooze between her legs. She pushed through the thick vegetation and clambered up a damp hillock to a spot where she could look out over the hills and the town below. The sight that met her eyes made her gape, and she dropped her smoke onto the earth.

The air was completely still, and in the faint first glow of morning she could see them: tall, perfectly straight columns of mist rising from every bit of water in the landscape, dozens of ethereal white pillars stretching up from ponds and inlets. Looking out to sea she saw more mist there, heavy, threatening, roiling in place. She'd never seen anything like it before.

After a while she crouched down to get her roll-up, and she noticed the ants. They were everywhere, crawling over everything, a black sea surging around and over her feet. None of them were biting, though, all focused on something more important than a human in their territory.

Her trance was broken by a sudden wail from behind and below the hillock. Frankie was awake and perturbed. With a final look back at the freakish pillars of mist, Katherine turned and made her way down to the camp.

§

Belinda was the first to shower. Still wrapped in a towel, she went out onto the balcony to get her clothes from where they had been drying on the line. Even now, thanks to the humidity, they were still a bit damp, and she sighed and unpegged them. Then, her attention caught by motion on the balcony rail, she went over to look.

Ants, thousands of them, scrambling over each other. Belinda had never seen so many. She watched them for a few minutes, then shrugged and went back inside to dress.

When she came downstairs, Belinda found her brother and his fiancée sitting up on the couch, still shrouded in blankets, blinking at the morning.

"Mo-or-ning!" she sang, smiling and pirouetting in front of them. Steven licked his lips, and Sarah smiled a tired return greeting. Belinda went round the room, turning on lights and fans.

"It's gunna be a hot one," she commented, glancing out at the dark, gloomy sky. "Rain, too—the ants are going crazy."

She flicked on the little radio her parents kept on top of the fridge and listened to the news. Yesterday's cyclone was expected to dissipate and move out to sea. Relieved, Belinda began to break eggs into a pan.

"Yes please," said Steve, appearing beside her in pyjama trousers too small for him. Looking round, she saw that Sarah was wearing the pyjama top over a pair of shorts. The fine hairs on her legs caught the morning light. As Belinda began frying the eggs, Steve launched himself at the kettle.

"Why don't cannibals eat clowns?" Belinda asked, prodding one of the eggs with a fork. Steve shrugged.

"Cause they taste funny!"

Her brother snickered and spilled the coffee powder.

"No eggs for me," called Sarah.

"Now *that's* Freudian," muttered Steve.

By the time Mary and Edgar came down, the others were washed, dressed and sipping coffee by the rattling fan.

"Thanks for thinking of your father," commented Edgar, going over to make his own coffee.

"I did think of you, Dad. That's why I needed something strong to get me through."

"Ha ha."

Mary dropped into one of the kitchen chairs.

"Looks as though it's going to be hot and sweaty today," she remarked. "Any sign of Kathy?"

"She didn't come in last night," said Steve, watching to see his father's reaction. Edgar paused, then resumed his spooning. "We'd have woken up."

"You sleep alright on the sofa, Sarah?" Mary asked, solicitously.

"Yeah, fine. Your son snores something horrible though."

"Anyone gone to get the paper yet?" Edgar asked, looking pointedly at Belinda. She made a face at him and went to find her shoes.

§

Steve and his father were playing their annual game of Christmas Eve chess while the women cleaned up after lunch. Belinda was telling Sarah embarrassing stories about her fiancé's childhood.

"Farewell Aunty Jack, we know you'll be back!" Steve sang to himself, pushing pawns. Edgar's eyes glittered as he saw an opening. He enjoyed playing chess with his kids, though secretly this was because he still usually won.

"One of my friends has taught his computer to play," Belinda remarked, nodding over at the chess board. "He works at the uni, and during the holidays he programmed one of the machines there to understand the rules. Says it beats him regularly."

Edgar scoffed. "He can't be very good at it. You need intuition and imagination to play chess."

"I dunno, Dad. Brute force computation seems to do the job. It just calculates all the possible moves in a second or two, and chooses the best one."

Edgar laughed, then captured his son's bishop. Steve groaned. Belinda took Sarah to the bookshelves to dig out her brother's baby photos.

There was a noise from outside, a dirty wet blatt of sound, and rain began to fall.

"At last," said Mary, going round and opening all of

the windows and doors again. Then she gave a sudden scream. All of the others looked up.

"What is it?" asked Sarah, getting to her feet and going over. Mary was staring out through the screen door at the garden. Sarah followed her gaze, and saw the beetles.

There were hundreds of them: big, black and green beetles dropping out of the sky with the rain and wriggling madly in the sodden earth. More were flying through the downpour, clattering like clockwork toys and bouncing off the windows and doors. The air was thick with beetles.

"Jesus, come and look at this!" Sarah breathed. The others came over and watched, open-mouthed. Other insects were appearing now, zinging madly through the rain and battering themselves senseless against the screen. Mary jumped back as a particularly big beetle ricocheted away from directly in front of her face.

"What the hell is going on?"

There was quite a wind now. Gusts hurled the rainwater sideways at the glass. "You reckon it's the cyclone? I thought they said that wasn't happening?"

They looked at one another, nobody daring to answer. Then Edgar headed for the stairs.

"I'm going to fill the bath in case the water cuts off," he explained. "Mary, you and the kids start taping the windows, eh?"

They set to work. Belinda started taking the pictures from the walls and everything heavy or sharp from the shelves.

"Nothing's going to happen," said Mary. "It never does. But it's best to be sure."

She turned the radio on again, and fiddled through

the stations. Just music and sports. She shrugged and left it playing.

Belinda gave Sarah a mischievous grin. "Welcome to sunny Darwin," she joked. "This is why we fucked off outta here."

§

Frankie was kicking up a fuss as the rain hammered down on the huddled group.

"I want to go," Katherine repeated, hugging her child close to her and trying as best she could to shield him from the weather with her body. "This isn't going to let up for ages."

"Look, it's just a bit of rain," said Quartz, looking up from where he was ineptly trying to start a fire. The others, half a dozen girls and a couple of blokes, were sitting round under blankets, smoking and looking inertly unhappy.

"Give us the keys," Katherine demanded, stretching out her palm and holding it in front of Quartz's face. He ignored it, his bare knees in the mud, rain turning his grey shorts black. A runty flame flickered and died in the pile of sodden kindling. He swore and tried to spark another match.

"Muh!" protested Frankie, eyes screwed shut. "Muuuuuh!"

"Look, babe, just siddown and shuddup, okay?" Quartz snarled at Katherine. "Or look, I think there's a tarp in the Kombi, grab that if you wanna be useful."

Katherine clenched her teeth and kicked a slop of mud at him, and then she went to the van. There was no tarpaulin. She sat in the cab, clutching her howling son to her breast. Quartz circled his finger round his ear. *Mental*, he mouthed at the others.

§

"The cyclone is imminent. A few hours of organised family action can turn the odds your way. Keep tuned to radio or television news broadcasts. Batten down your house by making sure all doors and windows are securely fastened, Remove all pictures from walls and all table ornaments—these could be lethal."

The radio voice was replaced by a string quartet. Steve turned it down and went to the phone.

"There's something you're supposed to do with your windows, isn't there?" Belinda said. "Have the ones facing the winds open and the others closed, or is it the other way round?"

It was just after five o'clock. The family had spent the last few tense hours fiddling around in the sitting room, not doing very much in particular besides listening to the radio.

"Do you think we should go somewhere else?" asked Sarah for the third time.

"We can't! What about Katherine?" Mary replied, as she had before.

Edgar growled and moved his knight. "Bloody girl. Where the hell is she?"

"Do you think she's okay?"

"Of course she's okay, she always is! She's just giving us all a fright! Bloody irresponsible, that's all it is!"

Belinda sighed and got up, wiping her sweaty palms on her shorts.

"Look, I'm sick of just sitting around. I'm going to

pop down to the post office, check the weather reports. They usually pin them up pretty regularly. Might be a bit more specific than the radio."

"I'll go with you," said her father, getting up.

They went out into the freakish gloom, hunching their shoulders against the wind which whipped at the veranda.

"Wait!" Steve shouted, getting off the phone. He'd just tracked down an old mate at the local ABC studios. "Um, shit," he began. "Look, they think it's reasonably bad. It'll probably hit the town. Dead-on."

The others stared at him. Then Edgar, galvanised by the news, clicked into action.

"Okay, you kids, I want you to go *now*. Get in Belinda's car and drive the hell away from town. Your mum and I are going to wait here until Katherine gets back."

Steve and Belinda exchanged glances. Sarah shivered. "What if she doesn't?"

"She will, she's not dumb enough to stay out in this. She'll be home soon, I'm sure. Look, we'll take shelter here if things are getting bad. You lot just get away from here until everything calms down, just a precaution. You've got a radio in your car?"

Belinda nodded.

"Go on then, get going. The quicker the better."

Edgar and Mary came to the door, watching their two eldest children and Sarah climb into Belinda's pokey car. There was a flash of distant light from over the dark sea. Something malignant was moving and growing out there. Edgar ran back inside and returned with an expanding file filled with papers. It was the most recent draft of his book.

"I don't want to have to do all that again," he said, thrusting it at his son through the open car window. "Try not to lose it, 'eh?"

Steve nodded and Belinda fired up the engine. Edgar and Mary watched until they were out of sight.

§

From the front of the Kombi, parked between a pair of wind-whipped eucalypts, Katherine could see out to the waters of Beagle Gulf. Frankie mewed and kicked against her as most of Quartz's mates climbed into the back of the van, seeking shelter from the increasingly violent rain. She saw the first flashes of sheet lightning dropping like guillotine blades from the clouds.

By midnight the cyclone would only be five kilometres from land, and headed directly for Darwin. At four o'clock on Christmas morning, Katherine would watch Cyclone Tracy take the town and tear it to pieces. Huddled in the gloom, she sat and waited.

The Amazing Adventures of Ernie and Sal

He had a lot to work on, Edgar said. He'd never been busier.

The publishers wanted to know if he would commit to a new three-book deal, he said, but his agent told him they thought they could get a better offer elsewhere.

The garden was looking good, didn't Frank think, he said. All the rain was good for something.

He couldn't find his glasses, he said. He knew he had them here somewhere.

And Frank's aunt had told him Frank was working on something, he said. Some sort of comic, he believed.

"Er, yeah," Frank said. They'd already had most of this conversation two weeks earlier, the last time he'd visited, and then again on the phone a few days later. "A graphic novel."

A graphic novel, Edgar said. Sounded pornographic. Not that he was in any position to criticise, he said, not with some of the things he'd put in his books. Quite racy at the time.

"No, it just means a big comic," Frank interrupted. "A comic but with, like, the length and depth of a novel." This, too, he had explained before.

Oh, Edgar said. As far as he could see there was nothing at all that could compare with the depth of a novel, no other way to so perfectly capture the human experience. He wondered if Frank had thought of just writing a novel, and forgetting about the comics stuff.

"A comic's just words and pictures, Grandad. It's as old as art gets. You can do anything with it."

He supposed Frank might be right, Edgar said, though he was doubtful. And he also doubted there'd be any money in it. Still, Frank was at uni, he was getting his degree, there'd be time enough for that later. And what was it about?

Frank tried not to sigh. He was sick of explaining this to people, who were never as impressed as he hoped they would be, and he'd already explained it to his grandfather twice before, so he already knew what the reaction was likely to be.

"Well, in the 1950s it turns out Pol Pot and Che Guevara were both in Paris, right? Except their original names were Ernesto Guevara and Saloth Sar, right? Ernie and Sal, you see? Che originally studied medicine and Pol Pot studied radio engineering. So I have them meeting up and getting involved in all this weird post-war B-movie stuff. Aliens, leftover Nazi secret experiments, time travel, Cthulhu stuff, all of that. So it's like this crazy alternate history adventure. You know, changing history in the book."

Alternate history, Edgar said. He'd heard of that before. He wasn't as out of touch as people liked to think. He'd even contributed to an anthology once with a story about the English being beaten back into the sea in Sydney Harbour in 1788. But in any case, he said, all of this seemed a bit recherché, and he wondered how likely it was to find a market. But he supposed Frank was still at uni, and he had time to sort out what he was going to do.

§

p57: 3 panels in horizontal strips

Panel 1: Pitch black, just speech balloons.

ERNIE: I can feel a breeze from up ahead.

Panel 2: Pitch black.

SAL: Me too. Damn this torch!

"Rattle! Rattle!" sound effects to right of panel

Panel 3: Beam of light from torch going right, ERNIE's startled face caught in beam.

ERNIE: It's just a little bit further!

p58: splash page

Splash: ERNIE and SAL emerging from small hole in wall to left of page; the torchlight shows vast cavern, full of shadows. The place is piled full of treasure — loose bullion, jewellery, coins, gems, etc.

SAL: We've found it! The Nazi Gold!!!

§

Edgar looked at his notes, trying to work out what his train of thought had been. There were a lot of half-thoughts here, the writing trailing off before it got to the point. Then he found the photocopied map, its familiar but distorted coastlines, its wrong seas.

He'd been excited by the idea that, in the last Ice Age, it was possible to walk overland all the way from Tasmania to Papua New Guinea, that this was something an Indigenous Australian could have done, and in that first flush of excitement it had seemed as though there was a book in it. But now he realised the depth of the research required, the vastness of the imaginative leap needed to inhabit the mindset of someone in that time and place and culture, and how incapable he was of doing any of that.

"Mary?" he yelled into the empty house. "Mary? Have you seen my notebooks?"

§

p102
Panel 1: close-up on ERNIE
   ERNIE: Are you Finished?
Panel 2: close-up on ELDRITCH GOD, gibbering vilely
   ELDRITCH GOD: NOW THAT THE GRAIL IS MINE, ALL IS FINISHED
Panel 3: ERNIE From behind, ELDRITCH GOD looming over him
   ERNIE: Gimme back the cup you jerk!
Panel 4: Holy Grail slips out oF ELDRITCH GOD's hands; it looks embarrassed

§

Frank was reluctantly visiting his mother. Characteristically, after he'd been there half an hour, she suddenly announced she had to go out.

"Shopping," she said, and gathered together her things. From the depths of the house Frank could hear his laundry thumping away in the washing machine.

"You sure you need to do it now?" Frank asked. His mother shrugged the question off and scrabbled her car keys out of her handbag. She was not yet forty, but her attempts to make herself look younger actually made her look older. He wondered what he would do in the empty house. All the books had gone with him when he moved out, his mother never having been a reader, and the prospect of midday television or a back issue of *Who* magazine didn't appeal very much.

"Got nothing for dinner."

"Oh. Okay."

He watched her go—she was unable to leave a room without slamming the door, even when she wasn't in a mood—and then sat in the shadowy room for a while, listening to the washing machine and the traffic. Eventually he got up and wandered aimlessly around for a bit, poking his head into the familiar, boring rooms. His old bedroom was already filled with the junk his mother had no other place for: stacked fashion magazines, a box of styrofoam pellets, a full-length mirror with a crack across it, Frank's childhood toys. He picked up an old Transformer, his hands' muscle memory taking it from robot to Concorde while he snooped around.

His mum's bedroom was up the other end of the short passageway. There was a small, half-folded collection of male clothing on a chair in the corner, which he scowled at. His mother was a part-time secretary for a lower-echelon lawyer, and most of her relationships were with the men who trailed through the office with their ill-considered complaints and litigious impulses, their stories of being glassed in pubs or sacked unfairly for making personal phone calls.

Looking around, he saw that her jewellery box was open on the dressing table. It was the only thing of real value in the room, a nice oak antique that Katherine had inherited from her mother. He went over to it, remembering that he'd once found there was a secret drawer in it.

He lifted the box and slid his fingers around the underside until he found the piece of wood with a bit of give in it. He pressed it upwards, and there was a soft click. What looked like a part of the front was now protruding, and he was able to tug at it until the hidden drawer slid out.

He pulled it open and saw a manilla envelope. Frank was surprised when he lifted the flap and saw a glossy magazine, face down. He carefully extracted it and turned it over. It was an old softcore magazine with a 1981 publication date, with some former soapie star he didn't recognise baring her breasts behind some carefully placed type. He flicked through the pages, confused and aroused, and found his mother featured on pages twenty-three to twenty-eight, nude aside from high heels, and simulating sex with various parts of a Ford. The accompanying text called her Mandy, rather than Katherine, and quoted her as having expressed a series of unlikely opinions. She certainly seemed more agreeable than the person Frank knew.

He very much wanted to destroy the magazine, but also could not face any kind of conversation with his mother that doing this might lead to. In the end he carefully restored it to the envelope and put it back into the secret drawer.

§

p145:
Panel 1: ERNIE looks askance at the LITTLE GREEN MAN
LITTLE GREEN MAN: Take me to your leader!

Panel 2: ERNIE in close-up, raises an eyebrow

    SAL (off-panel): *Over here!*

Panel 3: SAL grinning, ERNIE Frowning

    ERNIE: *What do you think you're doing?*

    SAL: *He wants a leader. I'll be their leader!*

Panel 4: LITTLE GREEN MAN raises hand, seven fingers

    LITTLE GREEN MAN: *I come in peace!*

P146:

Splash page: viewpoint pulls back to show Sal's Terror Machine

    SAL (very small, next to it): *We'll see about that!*

§

Belinda nodded as her father monologued. The maps were spread out on the table in front of them, the corners lifting in the breeze from the front windows.

The continent was called Sahul, Edgar said, or at least that was what some people named it. Or Meganesia, he said. It was made up of Australia, including Tasmania and a lot of other islands, and Papua New Guinea, and a lot of other land now lost to the oceans. And here, to the north-west of Sahul, was Sunda, which was made up of Java and Borneo and Sumatra and Malaysia and beyond. These two huge landmasses, now broken up by the melting ice, and people could have walked right across them, Edgar said.

"I know, Dad. You told me this already."

But imagine a book about it, Edgar said. A novel, an

epic. A man, or a woman, some Aboriginal person fifty thousand years ago, walking from Tasmania to the New Guinea Highlands, in this world of megafauna. Snakes the size of buses, wombats the size of vans.

"Wombats the size of vans, yes, and the giant echidnas and the whatever elses. Look, Dad, you've been talking about this for years. Have you written anything yet?"

No, said Edgar, but listen, see here, this massive lake, but all salty, useless. They had hardly any fresh water. The population from before the Ice Age must have crashed, so many people killed by the cold and the aridity and the changed environment.

"Can I make you a cuppa, Dad?"

That would be nice, he said.

§

p202
Panel 1: A group of HOODLUMS stand in the shadows of an alley, their faces obscured by the darkness. One of them, the LEADER, steps forward.

LEADER: Alright boys, it's time to make our move. The boss wants that shipment of Plutonium, and he wants it now.

Panel 2:
The HOODLUMS draw their weapons and start forward.

LEADER: Remember, no witnesses. Take out anyone who gets in our way.

Panel 3:
A figure appears at the end of the alley,

only visible in silhouette.

    FIGURE (ERNIE): I wouldn't do that if I were you.

    Panel 4:

    The HOODLUMS turn to face the man, their weapons drawn.

    LEADER: Say, what goes on?

§

On the night of Australia Day they hauled four deckchairs onto the roof of the share house. It could be accessed by a makeshift trapdoor some previous tenant had cut into the corrugated iron of the veranda. As the fireworks exploded over the distant harbour, Frank and his housemates drank wine coolers and Coke, watching the sky light up. The percussive pop and crump of the explosions carried in the warm summer air: all the spectacle of the Gulf War which was on the news each night, but without Scud and Patriot missiles.

"To us!" they toasted, already drunk on their youth and independence. Frank and Letitia arm-wrestled while Tony coached. Letitia lost and blamed the mosquitoes. While she was inside getting the insect repellent, the others inflated the empty foil wine bladder and lobbed it into the next-door neighbour's pool. When it became apparent that their neighbours were not home to complain, they stripped down to their underwear, their feet bare on the still-warm iron, and climbed the fence to swim.

Damp hair trickling down his back, Frank floated in the shallows and watched the others splashing down the pool in an impromptu race, the black straps of bras tight across the girls' pale backs. Tony lost the race and had to do a nude lap of the pool. "The water's cold!" he protested, hiding his shrunken penis behind the wine cask.

Afterwards they sat along the pool edge, skin glistening in the starlight, dangling their legs in the water as they passed a joint back and forth. A perfect night, Frank realised. He told them how he'd got an interview with a publisher in a couple of weeks, someone who would look at his comics work. Maybe he'd finally have a publisher?

A perfect night. Then he told the others about his mum in the magazine and ruined it.

§

Frank was talking with his Aunt Belinda on the phone. Even though he didn't need to stay with her any more when his mother went missing for a few days, now that he had moved out of home and was theoretically old enough to look after himself, they still talked several times a week.

Belinda had been interviewing schizophrenics for a feature article.

"Seems like the voices telling you what to do move with the times," she told him. "Like, it was angel voices, then it was telegraphed messages from the ether, then it was radio signals, now it's microchips in the brain."

"CIA mind control?"

"There's a bit of that, yes."

Frank had once started making a zine repurposing the screeds from mad people and the religious handed out at train stations and in shopping centres, but had got too depressed to ever finish the thing.

"One weird thing, though," Belinda said. "I was talking to this one guy, interviewing him in a café, and I had to go to the loo. He seemed completely normal, too, all recovered, talking quite rationally and with calm distance about everything he'd been through."

"Yeah?"

"Yeah. But later, when I listened back to the tape, the whole time I'd been in the loo, he'd been repeating 'Belinda's going to the toilet, Belinda's going to the toilet, Belinda's going to the toilet!' in this weird monotone voice, his mouth really up close to my Dictaphone. You could hear the saliva."

"Fucken hell."

"Right?"

Frank laughed. "I want to see all the transcripts when you're done with this."

"It's not entertainment, Frankie. These people are mentally ill."

"Sure, of course, but I still want to read the transcripts."

"Ah, you're a little sicko."

"If I had a dollar for every time someone told me that. Hey, have you talked to Grandad recently?"

"Dad? Yeah. Last week, I think."

"Did he seem right to you?"

A cautious pause. "Not really."

"No. Not really."

§

p225

Panel 1:

ERNIE, SAL and the LITTLE GREEN MEN on the bridge of the starship, looking out at the vast expanse of the universe through the viewing window.

ALIEN CAPTAIN: As you know, we've been searching for our home planet of TrimpleFrant for decades now. Any luck on the scanners, Criin?

Panel 2:

CRIIN: I'm picking up a faint signal, captain. It could be TrimpleFrant. The frequencies fit.

Panel 3:

CAPTAIN (excited): Full speed ahead! We're going to be the first ones to set foot on TrimpleFrant in over a thousand years. Finally we'll solve the mysteries of our ancestors!

Panel 4:

As the starship speeds ahead, the crew begins to notice strange readings on their instruments.

CRIIN: Captain, I'm getting some weird energy signatures. It could be a trap.

Panel 5:

The CAPTAIN'S face falls as he realizes the danger they're in.

Panel 6:

CAPTAIN: Brace for impact! It's an ambush!

§

The child's face was pressed against the other side of the rippled glass set into the door of the doctor's office. Edgar watched the blur of skin and eyes, dazed, as the doctor's voice filled the air with probabilities and pronouncements.

The child suddenly pressed its lips to the glass, making a seal, and exhaled forcefully, cheeks ballooning. Edgar shut his eyes and then looked back at the doctor, who was holding out a piece of paper inscribed with several phone numbers.

"They may be able to help," he was saying. Edgar nodded and folded the paper into his pocket. "And there are some books I can recommend."

Edgar blinked. "Books?" he said.

§

The publisher's office was above a newsagent in the western suburbs. There were posters all over the walls, pictures of Captain Outback and The Drongo and Oz Mecha Force One from the company's various comics. The kid behind the desk looked about twelve.

"Um, I'm here to meet with Daniel Everdene? My name's Frank Gibbons."

The child stared at him for a bit, then screamed, "Daaaaaaad!" at the door behind him.

"What?" bellowed a voice from beyond.

"There's a guy here!"

"What guy?"

"Called Frank!"

"Frank?"

"Yeah, Frank!"

A sweaty and harried man appeared in the doorway.

When he saw Frank he seemed to relax slightly, but also looked more puzzled. "Did we have an appointment?"

"Er, yes. My name's Frank Gibbons? You said you were interested in seeing more of my work?"

The man squinted, then nodded. "Aw, yeah, no, that's right. You're the Pol Pot guy. Gotcha. Come in."

They sat in silence for a while as the publisher flicked through the pages. "You do your own inking?"

"Yeah. I used to use a pen, you can still see that a bit with some of the early pages, but now I do it with ink and brush. I'm going to go back and redo those earlier pages, make them fit the later style. So that when it's published..."

"Nah, I get it. I like it. Dark, but would reproduce well. Even on newsprint."

More shuffling. "Very pulpy writing style."

"Well, yeah, that's sort of the point. It fits the sort of comics being put out at the time, you know?"

A long pause. "But it just sort of does the same things, doesn't it? It doesn't, you know, transcend them in any way. It's just a pastiche with better art, really, isn't it?"

"Well..."

"I mean, you ever try to read those old comics? They're fucking horrible after about twenty pages. They do my head in."

"I would have thought..."

"I mean, people pretend they're important, and I guess they are, don't get me wrong, but I fucking hate them."

"But I was thinking..."

The publisher gave a heavy sigh and dropped into his chair, letting the pages he was holding slide back onto the desk. "Do you know what we've got lined up this year?"

"I, uh, I mean I got the December issue of 'Exit Wounds' a few weeks ago, saw the house ads at the back. Another 'Black Eyed Susans' miniseries, right? And the superhero books..."

"Yeah, all that's been binned."

"What? Why?"

The man sighed again. "You bought the first 'Black Eyed Susans' book? All four issues?"

"Yeah! I loved it. There's hardly any Australian crime stuff in comics at the moment."

"So you bought them. Okay. How many other people do you think did?"

"I don't know," Frank said.

"Fifty-seven bought number three, thirty-nine bought number four. That's Australia-wide. Got crates of returns of the fucking things sitting in my van right now. I was a guest at this convention last month in Melbourne. Couldn't even give them away. It was hell. I spent two hours at the signing table and only one bloke came up, had a first-issue 'Captain Outback,' and right after I'd signed it, I saw him take it off to one of the dealers to sell—and the dealer wouldn't take it! Weekend from hell." He shook his head. "You wanna know what we've got lined up for this year now? I'm drawing two-page porno joke spreads for 'Picture' magazine and caricatures of nude actresses for 'People.' You interrupted me drawing Greta Scacchi with her tits out when you came in today. That's how I'm feeding my son this year, mate." He waved vaguely at the door to the outer office.

"But what about the storylines that are still ongoing?"

"Fuck 'em. Listen, nobody buys Australian comics. Nobody here, nobody overseas. Unless you're one of those jerks who works for 'The Phantom' then you're stuffed."

The publisher reached over the desk and patted Frank heavily on the shoulder, a man trying and failing to be fatherly with a stranger. "Give it up, mate. I'm doing you a favour," he said. "This artform will ruin your bloody life."

§

p232

Panel 1:

SAL: **What do you want from us?**

ALIEN CHIEF: **We will not tolerate the intrusion of outsiders on our world. You must be punished for your transgression.**

Panel 2:

ERNIE: (to himself) **There has to be a way out of here...**

Panel 3:

ERNIE: (to SAL) **I have an idea. If we can disrupt their power supply, we might be able to escape.**

ALIEN CHIEF: **Silence! Take them to the Pit!**

§

It was a rare cool February day, with fresh rain clinging to the bus windows. Frank half read a comic and half dozed on the trip to his grandfather's house, head leaning against vibrating glass. Wollstonecraft was a long way from his share house...

Edgar's street was quiet, young trees drenched and swaying. Frank pushed open the front gate and strolled up to the front door. Nobody answered when he knocked, but he could see Edgar's car in the carport and there were lights on behind the pebbled glass of the front door. He tried the handle. It was locked, but he had a key for emergencies.

"Grandad?"

The lights were on inside, and a radio played in another room, some sort of country-hour program. The old fridge hummed in the kitchen. There was no other sound.

"Grandad?"

He inspected the kitchen in passing. A half-full bottle of red wine sat upright in the sink. A broken wineglass lay next to it, fragments of glass gleaming in the wet.

"Anyone home? Grandad?"

He peered through the door into Edgar's study. In the corner was the jumble of boxes his grandfather had been collecting for years, full of old photographs and bits of documentation about the family. The base elements of another unwritten book. A pile of Edgar's own books was stacked neatly on the otherwise empty desk. A piece of paper was folded to stand upright on top of the stack. "Belinda" was written neatly on it, in black felt-tip.

"Oh shit," Frank muttered, going to the bedroom.

Edgar was in there, tangled in the white sheets. He was naked, at least above the waist. He lay, head back on the pillow, eyes closed. Another empty wine glass was on the floor, tipped over. The pill bottle was there too, also empty. There was the faintest faecal scent in the air.

Frank held his hand over his grandfather's face, felt no breath. He held Edgar's wrist, was stunned at the feeblest pulse of blood beneath her fingers. He dropped the arm, shocked, then held it again. The pulse was already weaker.

For a moment Frank stood there, looking down at his grandfather. Then he left the room, going down the passage and out the front door again. The sun had cleared the clouds a little, giving everything an almost wintry glow. He sat down on the edge of the veranda, feet in the damp soil of the garden. A young couple went past with a Labrador, which grinned at him and then moved on.

Frank waited five minutes, then slowly got to his feet again. He went back inside and called an ambulance.

WARNING:
CAPE DOES NOT
ENABLE USER TO FLY

Batman's Mother

It was hard to talk on the phone with Batman rampaging through the kitchen, making car noises with her mouth.

"Could you do that somewhere else, Elise?" Mei asked.

"Batman, not Elise."

"Either way, can you do that somewhere else, sweetie?"

"Who are you talking to on the Batphone?"

"Ugh. It's your dad."

Batman's eyebrows rose. Her costume was fairly baggy and frayed, having come out of a Royal Show showbag and seen a lot of action since. "Is he coming this weekend?"

"Maybe. We'll see. He might be working."

§

Before Batman was born, Mei had written and published a novel with a university press. It was heavily based on the poor life decisions of her older brother, and it was a testament to his blithe indifference to anything but his own sex life that he had never read it and so did not know this. It had been widely ignored, being reviewed only in the tatty newsletter that was all that was left of that same university's student newspaper.

Her editor had suggested that she might do better next time—ideally with a different publisher—if she capitalised on her Chinese heritage. Mei pointed out that her family had been in Australia since the gold rush in the 1850s, various of her great-great-great- and great-great-great-great-grandparents having been miners or laundry women in Ballarat, Bendigo, and Maryborough, most of them landing in South Australia and travelling overland to the goldfields to avoid the poll tax designed to keep non-whites out of Victoria.

"You could do a torn-between-two-worlds thing!" the editor enthused. "Traditional parents, family conflict, all that jazz."

"My parents are Melbourne hipsters."

"Nevertheless."

Even if this terrible idea had been a good idea, marriage and childbirth and parenthood and divorce intervened. One day she saw a couple of scuffed copies of her book in the 3-for-$10 bin in her local bookshop, thick black remainder marks across the top. It meant she could let go of writing, and that was an odd relief.

§

On weekday mornings Batman had to shed her costume, which she usually slept in, and assume her secret identity as Elise Gibbons, daughter of Mei Sun and Frank Gibbons and year one school student. This was usually a time of trial for both Mei and Elise.

"Can I wear my cape while I brush my hair?"

"No, you know it makes it hard for you to move your arms."

"Well, can I watch while I brush my hair?"

"Only for five minutes."

Elise was already hunting down Adam West on Youtube with Mei's phone. "This one has Catwoman."

"You know you don't have time to watch the whole thing."

"Can I watch half?"

After the negotiations, the organising, the packing, Mei was standing by the door. "We have to go, sweetheart!"

"To the Batmobile!"

§

Mei still worked at the bank, a job which had started as her own secret identity when she was really a writer, and which was now just her job. She was reliable, quickthinking and very good at disguising her absolute contempt for everyone above her in the corporate hierarchy, which meant she had survived the various rounds of cuts and retrenchments, and only had to do teller shifts every third day.

At lunch she ate at the nearby air-conditioned food court with Ruth, who'd been at the bank almost as long as she had. They watched the sparrows stealing scraps and crapping on the tables, and compared poor life choices.

"Elise is learning Mandarin at school, and keeps asking me what words mean, and I have no idea."

"Did I tell you I'm doing Yiddish on Duolingo? Again."

"Ha! Do you think you'll keep it going this time?"

"Hmm, yes, well. If lockdown didn't force me to, who knows how it'll work now with normal life in the way. But I feel like the sort of person who should know more than one language."

"Ha! Like I feel like the sort of person who should be

musical, even though I'm not. I have so many records!"

"Exactly! Oh, well, at least this time I might get further than the oys."

"The oys?"

"Yeah, you know, the oys. Like, there are various levels of 'Oy'," Ruth explained, her nimble fingers picking apart her vegetarian pizza. "There's your basic 'Oy', which is like mild dismay. You know, you drop your keys, you go, 'Oy!' Then there's your 'Oy vay', which is like your 'Bloody hell!' Then you've got 'Oy vay es meir!', which is pretty serious, like, 'Fuck me!' Then there's 'Oy gevalt!', which is reserved for your nuclear-level stuff. Things like, 'Oy gevalt! You want to marry my daughter?!!'"

§

Mei had married an older man who had already been divorced once, which even at the time she thought was probably a bad idea, and so it had proved. Frank Gibbons was a comics artist in a country that was too small to support an economically viable comics scene. His new project was always going to be the one that finally found a market, and it never was. His grandfather had been a successful and well-off novelist, which was possible in the twentieth century but had given Frank inflated ideas of what was possible in the twenty-first. In the end Mei realised she could support herself and Elise on her bank income, but she could not also support a man who was convinced his projected thousand-page time-travel graphic novel about Gallipoli being wiped from history was going to be a bestseller. And there had been other problems.

"We could have dinner," Frank suggested. "Talk

about things."

"We're talking about things now," Mei said, putting the phone on speaker as she struggled to lift down the casserole pot. "And I'm not going to make you a meal, and you have never cooked anything edible in the whole time I've known you."

"No, I mean, I'll take you out somewhere. Somewhere nice. You choose. I'll pay."

Mei frowned. She could see Batman outside, throwing a tennis ball for the Bathound. Now that it was daylight saving time she refused to come in until the mosquitoes started to bite.

"I don't know," she said, managing to snare the pot handle with the tips of her fingers. "Adulterer."

"Do we have to do that now?"

"Oh, I'm sorry if it's inconvenient to bring that up."

"Fucken hell, Mei, can't we try and sort this out? You're my wife!"

"Yes, well, you remember that now,"she said. "Fat lot of good that does me now."

§

She saw an ex-boyfriend on the news: Carl, Frank's cousin. She and Frank had met at a nightmarish Gibbons family gathering she'd been talked into attending by Carl, when their relationship was already falling apart. Frank had seemed funny and different and appropriately sarcastic about everybody else at the party, and afterwards they'd gone out drinking together.

Now Carl was a Red Cross aid worker, which was entirely in character, and had also been captured by militants on the Syrian-Iraqi border in confusing circumstances, which was also entirely in character. The Australian authorities were expressing their usual grave concerns and going through their usual impotent motions. When his name was mentioned on the news Mei recognised it straight away, though it took a while to see the guy she'd known in the haggard, Unabomber-like photo they used.

"That man looks like Dad," Batman pointed out, noticing her sudden interest in the TV. The two of them had been building a model Batcave out of Lego on the floor of the lounge.

"He does a bit," Mei admitted. "They're related. I used to know him. He's, ah, let's see, he's your dad's mum's brother's son."

"Batman's son is called Damien," Batman pointed out.

"Well there you go then."

§

Frank took her to the Hilton for dinner. A waterfall plashed peacefully, a pianist tinkled gracefully, a man bellowed into his mobile phone about an upcoming demerger he was very excited about.

"Does Elise still think she's Batman?"

"Invariably. I had to buy her a new costume last week—the last one was in tatters. This new one has a label saying 'Warning: cape does not enable user to fly.'"

"That's pretty stupid."

"Exactly. As Elise pointed out, Batman can't even fly."

Frank laughed. "She's very like you."

They ordered. "Please make sure there's no nuts in that," Frank said to the waiter. "They could kill her."

"Thanks, Frank."

They sat in silence for a while, slowly drinking.

"How's work?"

"Fine. How's your mistress?"

"Agh, fuck, here we go."

"What was she, Korean? Vietnamese?"

"Does that matter?"

"Just like to know if you ever liked me at all, or did I just tick some fetish boxes."

"Shrew."

"Adulterer." The waiter had appeared with their entrées, and looked startled. "Not you," Mei assured him.

§

"So a disappointing evening, then?" Ruth asked at lunch on Monday.

"Ah, well, you'd have to expect something for it to turn out disappointing, wouldn't you?"

"Minisculey disappointing? Microscopically disappointing?"

"What's the smallest possible unit of disappointment?"

"Ha, I don't know. Like, when you chuck a ball of paper in the rubbish bin and miss, but nobody even sees so it doesn't matter?"

"Yeah, I like that. He was that amount disappointing."

"Your husband's a 'kadokhes.'"

"Are you only learning the insults?"

"Pretty much."

§

Sometimes after dinner Mei and Batman would watch epic fail compilations on Youtube. Batman liked nothing better than seeing babies throw up or adults falling down, and she would laugh hysterically until bubbles came out of her nose. Mei adored her hilarity. It moved her in a way she couldn't describe or contain, and it made her eyes brim.

Someone lost their pants in a water-skiing accident, and Batman laughed so hard that Mei had to go and get the Ventolin inhaler.

§

Mei knocked on the half-familiar front door and waited. After a little while she could hear somebody inside fumbling with the door-chain.

"Yes?" asked the woman. She looked old now in a way that wasn't just due to the passage of time. Worry and lack of sleep had made her face fall in on itself. Mei remembered that Sarah had been widowed only a few weeks before she'd met Carl, an accident (large bee in the car, big tree by the road).

"Ah, hi. Sarah? I'm not sure if you remember me? Mei? I used to go out with Carl?"

Sarah's face took a moment to clear. "Oh, my god, of course, Mei! Come in!"

The house was dark and slightly musty. "The place is a bit of a tip, I'm afraid," Sarah said. "This past week I've spent all my time on the phone." She stopped and looked back at Mei. "You saw about Carl, I assume?"

"Yes. I'm so sorry. Has there been any news?"

"Some photos. He seems to be healthy. They're saying he might be traded in some deal with the

Americans. I don't reallyunderstand."

"How long has he been with the Red Cross?" Mei asked.

"Oh, years. I was really proud of him. He could have been anything, one of those rich specialists, but he wanted to do humanitarian work. He's always been such a kind boy." She sighed and shook her head. "Can I make you some tea or something?"

"Let me," replied Mei. "The kitchen's through here, right?"

"What a memory!" said the woman, absently. "Sorry, I need to look at my email, I'm expecting something from the government people."

"Of course, go ahead."

While she fiddled with mugs and hot water, Mei listened to the sound of the TV in the next room, playing the 24-hour ABC news on high volume. Sport, sport-adjacent scandal, Carl believed safe and well, politics, sport.

"I remember you were such a sweet, serious girl," Sarah said when Mei brought in the steaming mugs. "You were his first serious girlfriend."

"God, really?"

"It was years before he went out with anyone again. I worried, you know? You do worry. Do you have kids?"

Mei smiled. "A daughter. Elise. She's six."

"Oh, much better than a son! Do you have a picture?"

Mei nodded and poked at her phone. It was from Batman's most recent birthday, as she cut into her Batmobile cake.

"I liked Carl a lot," Mei said "I think he was probably just too earnest for me."

"Yes, I didn't think you two would last as long as you

did. It was fairly obvious he was a bit too intense for you."

"Ha, yes, well."

"And then you went out with his cousin? Frank?"

"That turned out to be unwise in a different way. We got divorced."

"So Frankie's your girl's dad? That makes us related."

"I guess it does."

"Both bloody Gibbonses. I always hated that name. Though my maiden name was Littlekoch, so you can see why I changed it at the time."

Mei laughed into her tea. "The least worst option."

"That covers most of my life choices," Sarah said, and sighed.

They talked on for an hour or so in bursts punctuated by silences. Sarah switched without noticing back and forth between talking about her son in the present and past tenses. Then the school called to say Batman had a temperature and in line with the COVID policy could she come and pick her up immediately.

Sydney Opera House in Flames

The fires had been closing in on the city for days, but Elias, effectively homeless and burdened by a giant malfunctioning pipe organ, had been trying not to think about it. When the power went out for the last time on Thursday afternoon, most of the other people in the place downed tools and went home. Elias was up in the organ loft when the lights died, nearly wedged in among the more than ten thousand pipes. He had a head torch for peering down into them, checking for blockages, so he was still able to see. He clung to the ladder and listened.

There were voices audible, echoing up from the concert hall below, but they grew fainter and soon went quiet. A door banged shut, then another. All he could hear now was a distant engine sound, perhaps an emergency generator kicking in, and the mysterious small sounds of the vast building shifting minutely against itself. And there was the sound, suddenly loud now that he became aware of it, of his own breathing.

Already unpleasant, the air began to heat up almost immediately, now that the air-conditioning had died. The organ loft was not a place designed for human habitation. Elias half climbed, half slid down the ladder. Out in the concert hall itself there was very little light—the green emergency exit signs, a few red LEDs on the scattered tools that had been left by the departed workers, a tablet someone had left running on an upturned plastic crate, its minute glow vanishing before it reached the acoustic petals on the ceiling.

Elias killed his torch and stood on the stage, letting his eyes adjust. The dim shapes of the seating boxes rose up to his sides, the stalls stretching up and away ahead of him, the empty choir space behind him between the stage and the bloody organ which had led to him being stuck in here today. Everything was tiered, a terrain of tripping hazards.

Fewer and fewer people had shown up to work each day this week. Homes were coming under threat from the fires, buses and ferries and trains were being cancelled because of the rolling power outages and fuel supply problems. Elias was reliably here each day, but only because he had nowhere else to go. He'd been secretly sleeping in one of the empty admin offices for the last three nights, after Neil had kicked him out.

Almost reflexively he tapped the phone in his ear. The four-hour-old message from Neil ("Come pick up your shit or I'll bin it!"), a stream of emergency alerts from Fire and Rescue, a missed call from a spammer. He turned the phone off to save its battery, pulled it out of his ear and pocketed it. He went over to the abandoned tablet, but as soon as he picked it up it scanned his face and shut itself off.

He picked his way across the cables of power tools and out through one of the side exits. It was just after three in the afternoon. In the stairwell he could no longer hear the generator, but the exit sign gave him just enough light to go down one flight and out onto the concourse. The daylight was shocking, boiling through the wide, high windows all along the Sydney Opera House's western side, under the vast sail-shaped roofing sections. The light was an angry red-orange, poisoned with smoke from the burning Blue Mountains. A low daytime moon was visible, full and stained red. He could clearly see the crosshatched scars from the Chinese accident.

Elias looked around, but there was nobody. He was alone on an endless expanse of expensive carpet starting to show the wear of the years since the last replacement. The building, always more showy than practical, was close to three quarters of a century old, and showing its age, hence the program of repairs he had been hired to be a part of. He slowly turned to his right and walked along past the empty bars and merchandise stalls, the toilets and storerooms with their doors propped open with sand-filled buckets. He listened, assuming there must at least be security guards around somewhere, but heard nobody. Only a couple of tourists were on the terrace outside, taking photographs of the Harbour Bridge backlit by the hell of the bushfire light. Seagulls clustered around the overflowing bins.

The admin offices faced north, looking out across the harbour waters to Kirribilli. The one he'd been sleeping in was halfway along the corridor. He slipped inside and locked the door, then looked up. The room's sole security camera was still as he'd left it, turned into a corner. The broom he'd used to adjust it was still lying across the desk, and the makeshift boobytrap of piled books was still untoppled in the path of the door. He'd not seen a cleaner all week, and it seemed nobody else had been in here either.

He climbed onto the desk and used the broom to push up one of the acoustic tiles overhead, then reached into the exposed cavity and pulled out his bag. It thumped dustily down onto the desk, tipping a vase of wasted flowers and brackish water onto the carpet. Elias stared at the puddle for a moment, then decided to ignore it.

He tried the light switch but there was no response. There was still plenty of malignant daylight, though, so he sat and ate a packet of dried apricots, wondering about his next move. He put his phone back in his ear and listened to the ultimatum from Neil again. He tried to ring his mum, but couldn't get a connection. Then, almost immediately he got a call from his mum's number. He steeled himself to deal with the usual "Elias, not Elise," rubbish, but all he got was silence.

"Mum, are you OK?"

Spooky laughter, chunky with compression artifacts. "Shaved teens," said a heavily processed voice.

"What?"

"You have a new message in your myGov Inbox!" Another shivery laugh.

Elias had never received a call from a Ghost before, and the skin on the back of his neck prickled slightly. Rogue artificial semi-intelligences loose in cyberspace, prank-calling their progenitor species and spitting back their nonsense at them. He listened as the opening bars of "Never Gonna Give You Up" began to play, then hung up and put the phone away again.

It was just after five o'clock now. He was feeling hungry, the apricots not having done much but gum up his teeth. Elias opened the office door cautiously, and slipped out into the empty corridor. On previous days he'd gone out at lunch to stock up on food for the evening, but he'd skipped lunch today and suspected if he left the Opera House now he'd not be able to get back in, and then where would he sleep? He had no money for a hotel room.

He went across the walkway to the other wing of the building and down a flight of stairs. The restaurant was silent, chairs upended on tables, the metal blinds dropped to hide the harbour view. Elias tentatively went in. Nobody seemed to be around. He tried the lights here, with no luck, but saw that the fridges behind the bar were still lit up. He went back there and ran a tap to get a glass of water. The pressure was low, and there was some sort of greyish matter visible in the stream, so he killed the tap and regarded the fridges. Some fancy beer he'd never be able to afford stood in gleaming ranks at eye level. He took half a dozen and put them into his bag. Then he went over to the wine racks, and found the motherlode. Penfolds Grange, Hill of Grace Shiraz, irreplaceable wines from vineyards now wiped out by storms. Four bottles and his bag was full.

The kitchen was through a side door, and provided a loaf of slightly stale bread, a tub of buffalo mozzarella, a slab of pâté, and the remains of a hanging prosciutto. Elias balanced it as well as he could on a big metal tray, added a couple of kitchen knives and some cutlery, then scarpered for the shelter of his office squat.

He slept badly that night, lying on the slightly too-short couch in his sweaty clothes. At one point he heard footsteps in the corridor, and somebody tested the lock before moving on. So there were still security guards on duty? The empty Grange bottle was now a hangover, and his fingers smelled of ham. When he used the office's small toilet the tank didn't refill after he flushed, and only a trickle of dirty water came out of the tap. He washed himself as best he could with paper towels and water from the spring water cooler. His crotch smelt intriguingly awful, so he applied hand sanitiser liberally and hoped for the best.

It was late morning now, and the power was still out. Presumably nobody was coming in to work today. His phone gave him more emergency service updates on fires and property damage and lives lost. The sky outside was just a glowing blanket of smoke now. There was nobody out on the terrace below, though he could see movement on several of the boats floating in the harbour. No ferries were crossing, and the traffic on the Harbour Bridge all seemed to be going one way. Even as he watched, there was some sort of collision—a puff of smoke and a tiny lick of flame—and everything ground to a halt.

He tried calling his mum and Neil, but neither answered. He wished he had his tablet—he could try to check the news, see what was going on, run a daily diagnostic on his hormone implant—but he'd left it behind accidentally when he stormed out of Neil's flat. None of the audio news feeds were synching up on his phone. Aside from the fire alerts, all he had was stuff from two days ago.

He heard someone walking down the corridor outside again, and froze. It obviously wasn't safe to go out of the office, or he might be kicked out by security, and he had nowhere else to go.

He spent most of the day on the couch, sleeping sporadically, desultorily reading a biography of Sibelius and some old arts magazines he found in the desk drawers. Much of the time he just stared at the end-of-the-world sky, absent-mindedly rubbing his palm over his beard, listening to the soft crunching sound. At dusk he ate the rest of the bread and cheese and then, in the darkness, lay there, worrying.

The next morning he resolved to go out of the office. He had no appetising food left, and was desperate for something other than booze to drink. The now un-flushable toilet was rank. Cautiously, he went exploring. The place seemed deserted. He crossed the walkway again, visiting the restaurant to get juice and bottled water, and used one of the luxurious customer bathrooms. There, too, the water dribbled away to nothing as he washed his hands and face.

Spooked, he eventually wandered upstairs to the opera theatre. Standing in the middle of the revolving stage with the fly tower above him, scenery backdrops hanging vast and motionless overhead, he finished his juice and wondered what he was going to do next. He dropped the empty glass bottle on the stage, and it rolled in a wide circle to fetch up against the stage curtains. Then the faint background hum of the generators stopped, the green emergency exit lights winked out, and he was in pitch darkness. In the distance, a voice distinctly bellowed, "Fuck!"

Elias ducked instinctively and stupidly, then cautiously shuffled backwards until he found one of the stage exits and went through into a corridor of closed dressing room doors. He had his torch still, so was able to avoid getting lost and injuring himself. But now he heard footsteps, getting closer and louder. He went into the nearest dressing room, closing the door slowly and quietly behind him. The room had a makeup table, mirrors, a couch and an upright piano. He could hear the footsteps still, and so he slipped into the gap between the piano and the couch, hunching down and turning off the torch so that no light would escape under the door.

Someone was banging around in the corridor

outside now, swearing. By the sound of it, they were repeatedly dropping something heavy. Elias felt a sudden urgent need to urinate. The thumping continued, then there was a strange hissing noise and a shout of anger. The pressure in his bladder was overwhelming. Elias dropped his pants and, kneeling, awkwardly pissed onto the floor by the couch. The stream of urine seemed to go on forever, and pattered against the carpet so loudly he was sure he'd be discovered. But, an eternity later when he'd finally finished, he realised the sounds outside had stopped.

He waited for five minutes, then lit his torch and stepped over the spreading mess he'd made to listen at the door. Nothing. He opened it slowly. There was nobody out there. Lying on the floor were a couple of big speakers and a fire extinguisher. There was fire retardant foam in ragged arcs across the walls and in puddles on the floor, with wet foamy footprints leading off down the corridor towards the opera stage.

His phone rang in his ear, making him jump. It was Neil's number. Nervously he answered. A Ghost began reciting memes at him in a passable imitation of Neil's voice, using chopped up and reassembled phonemes from missed call recordings of his ex's voice. Elias listened in fascinated horror for a little while, then killed the call. Now he could hear shouting coming from the stage, and so he moved off down the corridor in the other direction, his hand over the torchlight to mask it.

The corridor ended in a heavy fire door which had been propped open with a chair. Elias pushed through into reddish daylight coming through the northern windows of an open gallery area. A set of stairs led down to his left, and he went down them, intending to head back to the restaurant to stock up on supplies before deciding what to do next.

"The fuck?" said a quiet voice behind him. He turned to see a man in a Sydney Kings shirt standing at the top of the stairs, holding an expensive looking augmented reality rig under one arm and a 3D sugar printer under the other. They stared at each other for a moment.

"Are you supposed to be in here?" Elias asked, deciding to bluff. "Security!"

The man boggled at him for a few seconds, then turned and ran. Elias listened to his fading footsteps, then continued downstairs. His body was wired with adrenaline and he felt oddly high, ready to fight or flee or fuck. "Calm the fuck down," he muttered to himself.

The stairs took him to another corridor, which led to a supply entrance to the restaurant kitchens. He pushed through the door at speed, already cataloguing in his mind the food and drink he wanted to grab, and then stopped still. There were already people in the kitchen. One man was sitting on the edge of a sink, drinking champagne from a bottle. Another was leaning over one of the stoves with an unlit cigarette sticking out of his mouth. What looked like the bottom and legs of a woman bending over were sticking out of the open door to the walk-in freezer. It smelled like gas.

"Look at all this stuff, it's still frozen!" the woman yelled, her voice muffled.

"What the hell?" said the man with the bottle, the only one to notice Elias.

"Ah, here we go!" said the man at the stove, and a gout of flame suddenly shot up from one of the gas cookers, setting fire to his cigarette, his face, and the tea towels left hanging to dry on the edge of the range hood.

"Holy shit!" said the man with the bottle. He started to run out of the room, tripped over something, and fell forwards. There was a loud chock sound as his head hit the corner of a counter, and he lay still. Blood began to pool under his head. The woman screamed and ran over to the burning man, who was reeling around the kitchen. The flames, fuelled by the gas in the air, were already spreading impressively, one of the burning tea towels having dropped onto the counter and the other onto the floor. With a series of tiny pops the heat sensors in the overhead sprinklers went off, but only a small trickle of water came from each one.

Elias tried to help the woman with the burning man, but she hit him with something she was still holding from the freezer—a frozen leg of lamb wrapped in plastic—and sent him sprawling. He tripped over the man with the broken-open skull and fell heavily onto the bloodied white tiles. When he got to his feet the whole room seemed to be burning, and the woman was hauling the unlucky smoker out through the door Elias had come in by. Elias now ran out through the other exit, into the main restaurant. Fresh oxygen flooded in through the two open doors, feeding the flames.

The double doors leading to the outdoor eating area by the harbour were locked. He picked up one of the steel-framed chairs upended on a dining table and whanged it into the glass. It bounced off, but left a sizeable crack bisecting the door vertically. He hit it again and again, until suddenly the door dissolved into fragments, some of which went into his arms. Ignoring them, he threw the chair out through the gap and then scrambled through himself. The air outside stank of smoke, and for a moment he assumed it was from the kitchen fire, but then he realised that the trees and houses across the water were burning too. The sky was smoke and a patch of glowing red overhead was all he could see of the sun. Elias turned back and saw the flames from the kitchen were now expanding into the restaurant, licking up the dark wood panelling and popping the bottles behind the bar.

There was a small yacht floating some way out in the water. He could just read "BIG JOHN'S BIG ONE" lettered down the side. Elias couldn't see anyone aboard, though they could have been belowdecks. The phone in his ear began to ring again, and he pulled it out and shoved it into his pocket. He trotted the hundred or so metres along the boardwalk to where a set of concrete stairs led down to below water level. From this angle he could see the Botanic Gardens behind the Opera House were on fire too, black smoke streaming north through the gaps between the hideous apartment buildings overlooking Circular Quay. And then something exploded inside the Opera House itself, glass blowing out from the foyer level above the restaurant.

Elias stepped off the bottom stair and plunged into lukewarm water, the surface glittering with plastic and smoke particles embedded in the murky algal bloom. He started dog-paddling out towards the boat. Sydney burned all around him.

ABOUT THE AUTHOR

James Morrison was born in Adelaide, Australia, on unceded Kaurna Country, and lives there with his wife, daughter, and dogs. For many years he has written about book design as the Caustic Cover Critic. He has too many books.